I0726929

Stories of the Veil

GUARDIANS OF THE VEIL

GUARDIANS OF THE VEIL
STORIES OF THE VEIL

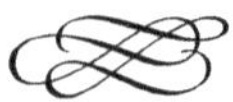

PEPPER MCGRAW

PMG Publishing

P
M
G
Publishing

CONTENTS

CHAPTER 1

*K*alina was tired.

A thousand years, plus five hundred more, were both a gift and a tragedy.

A gift that she had so many years to be a part of something greater than herself and a tragedy because those years were a tiny droplet against the vast lifespan of the Fae.

Perhaps if she'd never met him, never known he existed in this world, she could have gone peacefully, filled with joy that she could offer herself in sacrifice for the good of Faerie.

She had met him, though, and there had been no joy or peace ever since, just sorrow and loss.

In the beginning, it wasn't so hard to ignore the yearning for her fated mate, the pull of that matebond that somehow grew stronger and deeper the longer they were apart.

Now, though, four hundred years since that first fateful meeting, she was tired and she *yearned.*

She burned for him in much the same way she imagined they would soon burn for Faerie.

The end wasn't yet upon them—their thousand years, that droplet of time that now wound down at an ever-increasing rate, that droplet that once seemed endless, now almost completely spent.

She wondered if it would be much different when the time came, a mere thirty-one days from now, for them to meet their destiny—him at the Eastern Veil, her here in the West—when they burned for Faerie like they currently burned for each other.

She had always believed that when the time came, she would be ready to throw her life force upon the Veil, to burn herself to ash in sacrifice.

She discovered, however, that she was not, suspected even that she would *never* be ready, not when it meant her fated mate would be burning half a world away, the two of them without even a single kiss to send each other into eternity.

She might be both Fae and Guardian-born, but in this, she was not the honorable Fae of Legend, the ones who had gone before her, the ones who would go after.

Though she walked among the greatest Fae of her

generation, she felt none of the honor they did as the spiral of destiny swept ever closer, bringing with it, the sharp tang of grief.

Thorne was tired.

The end approached at an increasingly swift pace and though he had agreed four hundred years before that the good of Faerie was more important than one simple matebond, four centuries later, he knew he'd been a fool.

Four hundred years they had wasted when they could have set the world afire with their passion.

Four hundred years they had lost.

They had squandered the greatest gift any Fae could ever hope for and it was not to be chosen as Guardian of the Veil.

They had chosen honor over their fated bond and now, as their destiny spiraled ever closer, he had no memory of why.

Why they had considered honor and duty to be more important than the gift they had received in each other.

Now, a mere thirty-one days from when they would be called to burn their life force upon the

Veils of Faerie, he had little patience for duty or for honor.

Nevertheless, when the request for a meeting came from the Commander, Thorne found himself striding down the corridor, headed for the offices, no thought but to fulfill his duty once more.

Fifteen minutes later, he was certain he was hallucinating. "You want me to what?"

"I am so sorry, Thorne." Commander Agarra had a haunted look on her face. "I know this is not how you envisioned your thousand years of service ending. You should by all rights be here with your brethren, burning with them upon the Eastern Veil, entering eternity at their sides. Unfortunately, the Western Veil has lost two of its Guardians in as many days. As you know, we must maintain the balance at all costs."

"If you send me, we'll be a Guardian short at both Veils," Thorne protested.

"We have two from the Reserves coming, but they will not be as prepared as any one of the Guardians. It is better for us to send an experienced Guardian to the west and to have one inexperienced Fae from the Reserves at each border site."

"We'll still be unbalanced," Thorne said. "The west will have two not connected to their whole, not part of the one."

Commander Agarra nodded. "It is terrible timing.

The two Reserves will be trained hard from the minute they arrive at both sites, but it is our best option at this point."

Thorne just stared at her. Did she realize what she was asking of him? Of all the Guardians, why would she choose him? "Why me?"

She sighed. "This is not a decision taken lightly. We consulted three different Seers. They all said the same thing. Send Thorne Evaria to the West, and so, though it breaks my heart to ask this of you, Thorne, to ask it of any of our Guardians, I must do so anyway. Will you go and burn on the Western Veils, though you know them not, for the good of Faerie?"

CHAPTER 2

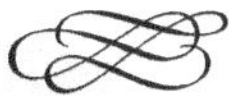

As far as Thorne was concerned, it was a miracle.

Though he knew it would be a true test of his control and his honor, he would not have to perish half a world away from his love.

He would be there, to burn with her, to hold her close as their thousand years came to its destined end.

They would enter eternity *together*.

For this gift—this amazing, beautiful gift—he would be eternally grateful, even if he burned for the next thousand years.

Though to be clear, his gratitude was significantly outweighed by his outrage at the vagaries of fate.

Kalina should not belong to all of Faerie the way she did. She should be *his*. The thought that she wasn't enraged his more primitive side, bringing the legendary feral Fae to the fore.

Ours, the beast roared every time they met.

In the beginning, they had done everything they could to minimize those encounters, but as the years went by and their yearning for each other grew, they'd known it for the losing battle it was, and so they'd spent centuries both feeding their bond and starving it.

When the yearning became unbearable, they would meet and spend time in each other's presence, never touching, never growing the bond, yet sustaining it nonetheless.

And so the tragedy of their mating became a roar in the background of their lives, a roar that grew in magnitude with every encounter.

That a Guardian should have a mate at all, let alone another Guardian, was an outrage, a slap in the face from Fate herself. Fate who had deemed them both Guardian-born.

As Fate now sent him traveling across Faerie to the Western Veil where his love resided, Thorne could not help but wonder whether this was yet another slap in the face—Fate deciding to torture them both one final time—or if instead it was a message warning them not to squander any more of their days together.

The latter, he decided, as the compound that housed the Western Guardians rose in the distance, as the bond that connected him to his mate throbbed in joy as he rode ever closer to his love.

Kalina froze where she stood. She could feel—

She turned and stared in the distance.

Ever since Yelena and Norrick fell, there had been talk of replacements from the Reserves.

However, only one replacement had arrived and rumor had it, they were sending a second from the Eastern Veil.

Surely not though.

They could not possibly be so lucky or so epically doomed.

Her matebond, however, told her otherwise.

It throbbed in rhythm to some unknown song.

She closed her eyes and listened.

A rider.

On horseback.

The rhythm of pounding hooves.

Her eyes flew open.

Thorne.

Before she even realized what she was doing, she was on the move.

She raced through the compound, ignoring the Guardians who turned and called out her name, demanding where the danger was.

No danger, her heart whispered, though she had no breath to speak.

No danger, my love.

She leapt over a cart that moved into her path at the last minute, her feet flying, not even grazing the top of the wagon.

She landed and raced around the group of Guardians who had stopped to watch her approach.

There.

She hurtled past the Guardians at the gates, ignoring their calls, their questions.

Thorne was on horseback, the two of them racing across the bridge, the hooves of his mount filling the air with a drumbeat that mingled with her heartbeat, the throb of the matebond, a song only she and her love could hear.

Halfway across, he leapt from his mount and she barreled into his arms.

He caught her up and swung her around before setting her down and leaning his forehead against hers to stare into her eyes.

"Thorne," she whispered. "You're here."

"They transferred me, my love."

"Do they know what they have done?"

He shook his head. "I doubt it." He glanced toward the gates behind her. "I'm sure they're beginning to figure it out, though."

Kalina didn't turn to look. She knew behind her stood her brethren, the Guardians she'd served with these past thousand years, the Guardians with whom she would perish.

But not alone.

Not halfway across the world from her love.

Instead, he would stand at her side and they would fly into eternity together.

"Come, my love." Thorne took her hand in his, settled his other hand on his steed's neck and led them both the rest of the way across the bridge.

Though it was madness and though it revealed entirely too much to the Guardians of the Western Veil, when Thorne saw Kalina racing toward him, a radiant joy upon her face, nothing, not even the sword of Galadriel, could have stopped him from meeting her halfway and lifting her into his arms for the very first time.

He would accept whatever consequences came, but no one would ever separate him from his love again.

Not even the entire Guardian Force of the Fae.

"Let me see if I understand this." Commander Helier had been pacing before them, back and forth, for an untold number of moments, not speaking, just pacing and every once in a while, shooting them a glance through eyes lit with both hope and despair. "You two are fated mates."

"We are," Thorne said, a song of hope in his heart.

"Yes, Commander," Kalina said at the same time.

"And how long have you known this, Kalina?"

She glanced at Thorne, then back to the Commander. "Almost four hundred years now, sir."

The Commander froze in place, then turned to face them both. "Four hundred years and you have said nothing. You have not sought to end your roles as Guardians nor have you requested to serve together."

"End our roles?" Kalina exclaimed. "We would never."

"It is a matter of honor, sir," Thorne said. "We decided long ago that we would fulfill our purpose for the good of the Fae. It is what we were both called to do."

"Yes. You are Guardian-born, but we could have found replacements for you both. Now it is too late."

"We do not wish to be replaced, Commander," Kalina said. "We are here to serve the Fae. We are simply overwhelmed with gratitude that we might end our days together."

"Then why not request to serve together?"

Kalina shook her head.

"The bond is too strong, sir," Thorne said. "The longer it existed, the stronger it became, and the greater the risk we would not be able to hold our vow to protect the Veils. It was better to stay far from each other."

"For the good of Faerie," Kalina said.

"And yet, you are here now, Thorne Evaria."

"Fate has called me here, sir. I could not ignore its demand."

"Yes, yes. I was fully briefed about the Seers. What I do not know is what it means, though I fear the fate of all the Fae lies in the balance."

"It is not forbidden that Guardians have mates," Thorne pointed out, "simply that they do not."

"There is something to be said for tradition," Commander Helier snapped, then shook her head. "No, you are right. It is not forbidden. It has simply never happened. In thousands of years of Fae history, not one Guardian has ever met their Fated Mate. Not once. And yet, here you two are. Fated Mates who met four hundred years before they would be called to burn for the Fae."

She turned and paced back and forth some more, clearly thinking on the dilemma. Finally, she stopped and faced them.

"Go. I am sure the two of you have much to catch up on. Be together—but not too much together, at least not until I have a better understanding of what we're facing. I shall consult the Seers and the Fae Council, the Queen of Fae, and all the rest, and we shall see where we end up."

"Yes, Commander," Kalina murmured.

Thorne gave a short bow and caught Kalina's hand in his.

Turning, they left the Commander's office together.

The moment the door closed behind them, Kalina turned into Thorne, burying her face in his neck and inhaling his scent.

He wrapped his arms around her, and there, in the quiet corridor outside the commander's office, they stood in each other's arms, just holding on.

Finally, long moments later, Kalina pulled back.

"Come. I'll introduce you to the other Guardians."

They didn't have far to go, for the moment they stepped out the front door of the administrative building, they faced a gathering of Kalina's fellow Guardians.

They had accompanied Kalina and Thorne in silence, all the way from the gates to the offices. They hadn't tried to speak or to delay them, not when everyone knew they needed to report straight to the Commander, but now that duty was done, the Guardians were waiting.

Mitaru was the first to speak. "Kalina," he murmured. "Thorne. I am so happy for you both, that you will be together as we approach the end." He hugged Kalina, offered his arm to Thorne in a warrior's hold, then turned and stood at Kalina's other side to face the rest of their brethren.

Shaliah stepped forward. "He is why you've been increasingly unsettled, isn't he?"

Kalina nodded. It was unusual for a Guardian to not find peace as their time wound down. She had seen her friends' concerned glances, but had been unable to explain.

"This is Thorne Evaria, my mate."

Thorne lifted her hand and kissed the back of it, all without turning his eyes from the Guardians facing them. "I was transferred here in response to the loss of two of your own. I am truly sorry for your losses, but I am overjoyed to know that I will be able to end my days at the side of my beloved."

Those were clearly the right words and tone to take, for the Guardians, who had stood frozen, rigid neutrality on every face, relaxed into smiles and began to step forward, introducing themselves and welcoming Thorne to the fold.

Kalina had never been so grateful for the incredible camaraderie that came of being a Guardian. That sense of belonging, of being part of something bigger than herself, of being just one vital piece of an unending, enduring whole, was something she had never and would never take for granted.

But now, after introducing her mate to the Fae she had served with for a thousand years, she knew a small part of her had not quite, even after so many years of service, understood what it was she had gained in this role. Not until that very moment when her closest comrades stepped forward to embrace Thorne as one of their own, simply because he was hers.

Now, hours later, after enjoying lunch with her unit and after giving Thorne a tour of the entire compound, the two of them were finally alone.

She led him outside the compound, down a long path deep into the forest, toward her favorite place in all of Faerie, the Dyagonin Falls, a place she'd never thought to share with her mate.

When the pounding song of the Falls came to their ears, Thorne smiled. "I've heard of these Falls, that the sounds they make are legendary, that they sing to the ears of the Fae. I never really believed until now though."

"Wait until you see them," Kalina advised. "You will never doubt again."

A few moments later, they rounded a curve in the pathway and the forest opened up, revealing the majestic power of the water as it hurtled over the top of the cliff and rushed toward the lands below.

It landed in a thundering roar of sound, again and again, water rushing past, the song of the river and the Falls bringing tears to Kalina's eyes.

This, right here, this moment was a miracle.

A miracle to witness the glory of this river with her mate at her side.

"Kalina." Thorne's voice was choked with emotion and she knew he shared her reaction to the true power that rushed through the lands of Faerie. He led her toward the bank of the river, unerringly heading for the boulder she always chose when visiting this site.

He helped her climb onto its surface, and though she had scrambled up this boulder tens of thousands of times all on her own, she accepted his help with joy in her heart.

Once she was settled, he hauled himself up and

joined her. He placed an arm around her back and nestled her close.

She rested her head on his shoulder and caught his free hand in hers.

There, facing the River of Dyagonin, hand in hand, they watched the water rushing by and settled into the peace and joy of being together at last.

Thorne wasn't ready when Nadim came through the trees hours later and informed them the Commander had requested their presence once again.

Still, he complied, as he always did.

He scrambled down from the boulder, then turned and lifted Kalina down as well.

Once she stood in front of him, he brushed a kiss across her cheek and whispered in her ear, "No matter what, we go into our destiny together, my love."

"Together," she murmured back.

He led her around the boulder to where Nadim was waiting. Then, hand in hand, they followed him back, walking side-by-side toward their destiny.

CHAPTER 3

FOURTEEN HUNDRED YEARS AGO

From the moment Kalina knew what a Guardian was, she dreamed of becoming one.

To be a Guardian was to live in the hearts of the Fae forever.

She wanted that. Perhaps it was arrogance or selfishness, or even both, to wish for more than she'd already been given.

To be born a Fae was to have millennia to learn and to live and to just *be*. To become the best at anything and everything you ever wanted in life.

And yet, she wanted still more. To know that her life had purpose and that when she left the world behind, her passing would have meaning.

She was an immortal Fae who craved even more immortality than she'd already been given.

To be a Guardian was to live in the hearts of the Fae forever.

From her earliest memories, she'd had this feeling that she was born for something important, something greater that waited just around the corner that she could not see, but could feel in every part of her being.

When she first understood the true nature of a Guardian at age twenty, it had seemed that unseen destiny was finally clear.

The disappointment had been keen when she learned she would have to wait until the age of majority to submit her name for consideration, and worse, would have to wait four additional centuries before she would be allowed to compete in the Trials to become a Guardian in truth.

Even her markings could not get her in early nor could they guarantee her a spot if she did not perform better than most of the other candidates.

Registration and the Trials happened only once every five hundred years and the two were separated by a span of four centuries, allowing candidates the time they needed to train for the Trials to come.

This was a double-edged sword for Kalina.

Her one hundredth birthday was mere days before registration for her generation began, which meant she would enter the Trials right after her five hundredth birthday.

Impatient to become a Guardian in truth, Kalina was thrilled she didn't have to wait hundreds of years to register.

However, it also meant that when she competed in the Trials, most of the Fae she faced would be older than her, some of them as many as four hundred years older.

Even knowing this, she wasn't willing to wait another five hundred years for her chance. She would simply have to train all the harder.

And so, on the very first registration day after her hundredth birthday, Kalina arrived at the gates of the Guardian Courts of the West as dawn etched its way across the horizon.

She expected to be among the first to arrive, but instead, discovered a long line that stretched around the building, hundreds of Fae waiting their chance to submit their names to become the Guardians of their generation.

In that line, Kalina met Mitaru and his sisters, Luna and Zara, who were only there to keep their brother company, and from what Kalina could see, to torture him a bit in the waiting.

They were directly in front of Kalina in line, which

meant the wait was not as boring as it might otherwise have been.

One of the girls held out a hand to a butterfly that flitted nearby.

It took Kalina a moment to realize the tiny markings across her shoulders and neck were moving and changing colors, as if they were still seeking their permanent forms and locations.

It happened so slowly that Kalina didn't even notice at first, but the longer they stood there, the more obvious it became.

It was a slow dance between forms, the markings morphing from leaves to flowers to butterflies and back again.

By contrast, the purple leaves trailing down the left side of her sister's face, marking her as a healer, and the black leaves on her brother's face, revealing him as Guardian-born, were stationary and unmoving.

A tiny sprig of what appeared to be minuscule blossoms were inching their way up toward the youngest's chin. If they continued their march, Kalina knew they would eventually settle upon the girl's face where most Fae markings settled.

Kalina had no such markings, at least none that had morphed and changed as she matured.

Instead, her markings had appeared two days before, on her hundredth birthday, tiny black leaves that trailed along her hair line from her left temple to the outer edge of her jaw. The marking meant everything to Kalina, a message from beyond that confirmed her hopes and dreams of becoming a Guardian.

Her family had been furious, her aunt, who had taken her in after her parents' deaths, in particular.

History, she had said with scorn and fury in her voice, *is like a plague reliving itself before our very eyes.*

It was the mark that had set her aunt off, a mark that to her, represented loss.

To Kalina, it was a mark of honor, one that very few Fae were blessed with anymore.

Once upon a time, all of the Fae had been born with markings like this girl's, ones that moved and mutated with the evolution of the Fae's power. They would settle around the Fae's age of majority and would remain stationary until the Fae's power surged again, something that had happened more frequently in the long forgotten past.

When the markings began to disappear from the Fae —so long ago few were alive who remembered those times—it had taken the Fae entirely too long to figure out what had gone wrong.

By the time they retreated from the lands of the mortals, much of the power of Faerie was gone.

It was then, several thousand years before Kalina was born, that the Veils were built, thousands of Fae giving their lives in the process. They burned themselves out, those early Fae, donating their life force to build the Veils as a shield between Faerie and the mortal world.

That shield, though, was not infallible.

When it became clear the Veils would not hold forever, that they had a lifespan of approximately five hundred years, there was no shortage of Fae volunteers willing to sacrifice their life force to protect Faerie and its magic.

From that very first generation of volunteers, tradition followed and the Guardians were born, a Force made up entirely of unmated Fae, for none wanted to see a mated pair fall.

That first generation of Fae volunteers gave way to the next generation and then to the next and then to the next again, each one devoted to that tradition of service and sacrifice.

And so it went. Every five hundred years, one generation was welcomed into the fold by a second generation while a third burned its life force to ash, all to ensure the Veils continued to stand strong against the mortal worlds.

After some three thousand years and six generations of Guardians lost, the magic of Faerie was finally strong once more.

The markings that had come first to the Guardians

and then to the royal family, were now appearing within the general population, to those like this young woman, proving once and for all, the full magnitude of their power was finally returning to the Fae.

Kalina knew this girl's magic would eventually become a blessing for all of Faerie, especially if the girl gained control over what leaked from her in tiny wisps of power.

Flowers bloomed where the girl stood and more butterflies came to rest on her neck and her hair.

"Luna," the other girl murmured.

"Can I help it if they like me?" Luna flicked a finger and a purple butterfly lifted from her shoulder and landed on her sister's. "There. Now you have one too, Zara."

Zara rolled her eyes.

"You know, Taru, this line is full of Fae." Luna glanced around, her eyes lighting on Kalina. "Including this amazing woman here." She skipped to Kalina's side and linked arms with her.

The butterflies followed, several of them landing on Kalina's shoulders.

She was charmed in spite of herself.

"I'm sure she is much more capable than you, Taru. Perhaps you should give up this silly dream to serve as a Guardian. What say you?"

Kalina grinned. How nice to already be thought of as capable, even if only to torture a brother.

Taru chuckled. "Thank you for your support, sister mine, but nothing you say shall convince me otherwise." He held out his right arm to Kalina. "Mitaru Verushi and these are my sisters, Lunastaria and Zaraniyah."

Kalina smiled and clasped his arm with hers. "Kalina Wyendeh, and I feel the same. Nothing my family ever said could convince me not to follow this path."

Luna sniffed in disdain. "Insane, both of you. Still I am quite willing to give you the benefit of the doubt and make you my very best friend anyway." She skipped around to Kalina's other side, butterflies still moving with her, and exclaimed, "I love the name by the way, but I think we need to shorten it. Because that is what we do in my family and you have been officially adopted. My name is Luna, you see, because Lunastaria is such a mouthful and my sister is Zara for the same reason, and Taru—well, he doesn't really deserve such an incredibly noble name as Mitaru. Your name is Kalina, right?"

Kalina nodded. This should be interesting.

"What do you think of Lina? Lovely, right?"

"Luna and Lina?" Mitaru said dryly.

Zara giggled and Kalina grinned.

"What?" Luna exclaimed. "I think it is *perfect* for two best friends, do you not agree?"

"No," Zara and Mitaru said together.

Kalina couldn't help but laugh.

"But imagine!" Luna exclaimed. "The two of us, traveling and shopping together, everyone calling us Lina and Luna. I think it would be marvelous."

"It would be ridiculous," Mitaru said.

"It would not!" Luna glared at her brother, but he just calmly waited. "Oh, very well. I suppose we could shorten your name to Kali instead, though I much prefer Lina."

Kalina grinned. "I love it. I've never had a short name before. I've always been Kalina, so this will be new. Actually, all of this is new. I've never had a best friend either."

Luna clapped her hands and gave a tiny hop. "Yay!" She flung her arms around Kalina and hugged her.

After a moment of surprise, Kalina carefully hugged her back.

Zara and Mitaru smiled at the two of them, clear looks of both indulgence and gratitude on their faces.

Kalina wondered why they seemed so grateful. After all, Luna was incredibly friendly. Kalina couldn't imagine anyone not responding to her with kindness and acceptance.

Then again, the Fae could be rather serious at times.

She wondered how many had tried to subdue the young Fae's exuberance.

Luna pulled away and exclaimed, "So, if you both make it into the Guardians—and I must say, though I want you to be happy, I'd really rather you not—you must promise me, Kalina, to look out for my incompetent brother. He's sure to get into a lot of trouble."

Thorne was among the first in line to sign up to become a Guardian the day of registration.

His brother, Tarek, and his best friend, Nako, accompanied him. Nako because he was also submitting his name and Tarek because he hoped to do the same in five hundred years.

"This is so frustrating," Tarek groaned for what had to be the tenth time that morning.

Thorne didn't give him a hard time about it, though, because he completely understood.

Tarek was almost ninety-nine years old, just over a year from the age of majority, yet not deemed old enough to submit his name. By virtue of a fluke of fate, he would have to wait until a year before his six hundredth birthday to apply.

It must seem terribly unfair to him when Thorne, by contrast, was able to submit his name at age two hundred and seven, and their friend, Nako, at one hundred ninety-two.

"Yes, but you'll have a substantial advantage," Nako pointed out.

Thorne barely stopped himself from rolling his eyes.

They'd already had this entire conversation multiple times on their way to the Guardian Courts of the East and several more times while standing in line waiting for the doors to open.

Yet, here they were, about to repeat it for the tenth, or possibly the hundredth, time.

"You'll have much more experience and a lot longer to practice," Nako said. "Once Thorne and I have submitted our names, we'll be training for the Trials for the next four hundred years. We'll share what we learn from the Training Camps and you can join us whenever we're practicing. By the time you register and complete your own training, you'll have had more than twice the training as some of the younger applicants."

Tarek just let out a huff of exasperation.

"Think of it this way." Thorne slung an arm around his younger brother's shoulders. "If you become a Guardian in the generation after us, Nako and I can sign up to be your mentors."

Tarek groaned and slid out from under his arm.

"Please don't. I'm sure I'll be much better off without your idea of mentoring."

"Our idea?" Nako exclaimed. "Are you implying we wouldn't be the very best of mentors?"

"I'm not implying anything. I'm saying it outright."

"How rude! Thorne, are you hearing this?"

Thorne grinned. "I am and I can't imagine why he'd insult us this way, especially since we've been mentoring him his entire life."

"Exactly," Nako said. "Teaching him how to ride a horse."

"How to fall off one, you mean," Tarek interjected.

"How to use a bow and arrow," Thorne said.

"In other words, how to accidentally shoot our father in his posterior," Tarek said.

Nako snickered. "That *was* hilarious."

"It wasn't," Tarek said.

"Oh, it definitely was," Thorne said. "And let's not forget our lessons in how to fight—"

"You mean how to take a punch," Tarek said

"Or how to climb to the roof of the tallest building in Elyria," Nako said.

"That lesson was about falling, not climbing," Tarek said.

"And how to woo the ladies." Thorne grinned as he pictured a young Tarek trying to flirt.

"That must be why I couldn't get a date to the annual Fae ball last year," Tarek said.

"I think it's obvious, based on the evidence presented," Nako said, "that we are truly epic mentors."

"Epically bad," Tarek muttered.

Training for the Trials began almost immediately after registration.

Each individual candidate was expected to train on their own, but they were also required to attend one Training Camp a year. By the time they arrived at the trials, each Guardian Potential would have attended four hundred Training Camps.

It became clear very quickly that these camps were used to separate the true contenders from those who would not make it to the Trials. It was obvious within a day of arrival at the first camp which candidates were training on their own and which were not.

Those who were not training, or who weren't training often enough, eventually withdrew their names and went on to pursue other interests.

Kalina was determined not to be one of them.

Therefore, she trained every single day, multiple times a day. Unfortunately, she was the only Guardian

Potential in her village, which meant she had no one to practice her skills on.

When she attended the first camp, one year after registration, this weakness became evident.

She did well on every independent challenge. She was faster and more agile than the majority of the Fae in attendance and listed in the top three on every individual test.

However, when it came to teamwork and to pitting her strength and skills against another—in fencing, in spellwork, in brutal fighting—she was clearly at a disadvantage. She'd had no experience defending herself or fighting a live opponent.

The only consolation was that she wasn't the only one in that position.

Mitaru, too, had been training on his own. Though there were a few other candidates in his village, they were several hundred years older than him and had apparently made it clear he wasn't invited to join them.

When Kalina discovered this, she suggested they meet to train together.

Though they lived a full day's ride from each other, this didn't stop them from meeting for a weekend of intense training every month. Mitaru always brought his sisters along, undoubtedly due to Luna's badgering.

They met in various cities throughout the lands, both in Faerie, and eventually, once short trips to the mortal worlds were approved once more, outside it, indulging Luna and Zara's love for traveling and for shopping.

Over four hundred years, it was more than enough time to forge the true bonds of friendship.

Thorne and Nako trained every day, sometimes multiple times a day, and Tarek joined them more often than not.

The annual Training Camps were a challenge at first, but as they became used to the types of tasks required of them and they got better at anticipating and developing an appropriate training schedule, the camps got easier.

As the day of the Trials finally approached, Thorne was more than ready to become a Guardian in truth.

"Do you really think you'll make it all the way through?" Tarek asked. "After all, there are a lot of candidates here and some of them look mean."

Thorne grinned. "We'll be fine, Tarek."

"If you say so. I'll be in the stands, cheering you on."

"Thanks, brother."

"Out of duty, of course."

Typical.

Nako snickered.

"I wouldn't laugh too much, Nako, considering we're not related and all. No duty to cheer you on. In fact, I think I'll cheer on whoever you're up against, in the hopes they knock you on your ass."

Nako chuckled. "You're doomed for disappointment on that one, Tarek."

"Only because I'm not allowed to compete yet."

Thorne and Nako both laughed out loud at that, mostly because it was true.

"It's a shame you can't compete, Tarek, but this will be better for Mother, not to lose us both in one cycle," Thorne said.

Tarek nodded soberly and held out his arm.

Thorne clasped it in a warrior's hold.

"Strength and wisdom, brother." Tarek turned to Nako, offered a similar warrior's hold, then said with a grin, "As for you, good luck."

And so it was that Thorne and Nako entered the Eastern Trial Arena, chuckling softly, with huge grins on their faces.

CHAPTER 4

The site of the Western Trials was on the outskirts of the old city of Pahzah.

Pahzah was a full three days' journey from where Kalina lived and four days from Mitaru's village. It was also one of the most beautiful and historic sites in all of Faerie.

For this reason, they made plans to leave a week before the Trials were set to begin.

Mitaru journeyed with his sisters to Kalina's village and met her in the town center, where most of the town residents had gathered to wish her good journey and strength of purpose for the Trials.

Her aunt and cousins weren't there, in a deliberate show of their disapproval of her decision.

Kalina wasn't bothered.

The only ones she really cared about would be journeying with her to Pahzah.

Still, it was nice the town had made the effort to show their support, especially in the absence of it from her family.

"Good journey, Kalina," Paero said as he passed her a bulging sack. "Just a bit of sustenance for the road." She knew whatever he had packed, it would be delicious, for he was an amazing cook and his mate a pastry chef.

"Thank you, Paero."

She secured the sack on Shahni's back, murmured a soft word of praise in the horse's ear, then swung herself up on her back.

She nodded to Mitaru and he led the way through the crowds and down the winding road out of her village. As they went, traditional blessings of "good journey," "swift feet" and "strong will" followed them out.

The moment the populated village was behind them and they faced open fields ahead, Luna, who was riding to Kalina's left, let out a cry of sheer joy and flung her arms wide.

"To Pahzah!" She clicked at the horse she rode and the two surged forward in a rush of movement.

"To Pahzah!" The others shouted and raced behind her.

It was a glorious way to start their journey.

Kalina grinned fiercely into the wind as she raced her friends and reveled in the freedom of the road.

Three days later, they were settled in rooms at the Pahzah Inn that Kalina and Mitaru had reserved almost ten years in advance, for rooms went quickly when the Trials approached.

Luna and Zara were pouring over their itinerary for the next four days, Luna focused on the shops she wanted to visit, along with any of the areas known for their wild animals, while Zara concentrated on identifying gardens, historical sites and museums.

The two had some good-natured arguments about whether the Noreli Hummingbird Garden was better than the fields where the cochari, known both for their beauty and their ferocity, hunted.

Eventually, they agreed they would visit both, which wasn't a surprise considering both adored anything to do with animals or nature.

Kalina grinned at Mitaru, who just shook his head in exasperation, something Kalina knew was only for show.

Mitaru indulged his sisters whenever and however he could and they both adored him for it.

Kalina knew, therefore, that the next four days would be exhausting, yet full of fun. Perhaps they would even be fun enough to alleviate the stress she felt at the approaching Trials.

She was confident in her abilities, but there were areas where she still struggled, and she knew the competition would be fierce.

At their last training camp the month before, there had still been more than four hundred hopefuls planning to compete in the Western Trials.

It was tempting to think this meant she would only be competing against those she'd trained with in the camps, but there was at least one other camp that fed into the Western Trials, not to mention the other ones that fed elsewhere.

After all the Trials were completed, the candidates across all of Faerie would be ranked and only the top five hundred would be chosen to become Guardians. Those five hundred would then be divided equally between the Northern, Southern, Eastern and Western Veils.

Kalina and Mitaru had discussed this over and over through the years and they had both agreed. It was not enough to outperform those of the camps. They had to be in the top echelon of the Trials, possibly even as high up as the top ten. It was the only way to truly ensure they would be accepted as Guardians.

"Oh, stop worrying, Kalina," Luna exclaimed. "You've been training for four hundred years. What more could you possibly do to prepare for the Trials to come?"

Kalina shrugged. "Maybe another practice session or—"

"No," Luna and Zara exclaimed at once.

Behind his sisters' backs, Mitaru was nodding fiercely in agreement.

Yes, another practice session or two would definitely help.

"There's nothing you can do at this point," Zara said.

"Exactly," Luna exclaimed. "If you're not ready now, you'll never be ready."

What a horrible thought.

"Now, come on." Luna leapt up from the bed where she'd been pouring over her notes of all the places she wanted to visit. She linked arms with Kalina and dragged her toward the door.

A glance over Kalina's shoulder showed Zara grabbing hold of her brother and hauling him in their wake.

"It's time for fun!" Luna hustled Kalina through the door and down the stairs into the courtyard that stood outside their rooms. "Let's go exploring!"

The next four days were wonderful.

The places Luna and Zara dragged them to invariably brought peace to Kalina's heart and soul, as they always did.

The hummingbirds flitting around in the gardens of

Noreli, the woods the girls dragged them through as they tested their abilities to communicate with the trees and the animals, and even the hours they spent wandering museums and historical sites honoring those long gone brought Kalina joy and peace.

Of course, that didn't stop Mitaru and her from practicing their skills along the way.

They practiced traveling through the trees, leaping from branch to branch, racing each other high above the forest floor as Luna and Zara cheered them on.

They tested each other's abilities with bow and arrow and magic in the maze of Correna, where they set for each other impossible tasks.

"So, here are the rules," Mitaru said. "You have to hit each target perfectly. Every time you miss a shot, the walls will move in. The only way they'll move out again is if you hit the final target in the perfect spot."

"You're diabolical," Kalina muttered as she studied the targets.

They were hanging high above the maze walls, sacks filled with leaves with a tiny red mark at the center of each. Despite being hung with magic, Mitaru had clearly ensured they would still sway and move with the wind.

This was going to be quite the challenge. "Time limits?"

"Thirty seconds between each target, five minutes to

complete the course. If you're late to a target, the walls will move in again. I suggest not being late."

Kalina sighed. "You know I'm going to get you back for this."

"Looking forward to it."

"Tell me when."

Silence for a moment, then, "Go!"

Kalina leapt forward and entered the maze at a run. She could only go by instinct, tracing the feel of Mitaru's magic that would hopefully lead her to the first—there!

Rounding a corner in the maze, she shot off an arrow and didn't even stop to see if it hit the target. She just kept moving.

The walls didn't shift, so she assumed her arrow hadn't missed. She made the next three shots, but then missed the fourth entirely when she realized Luna was sitting atop the maze, perilously close to where the target was.

Kalina jerked her aim to the side at the last minute and the arrow went wide, Luna laughing merrily in her wake.

"Are you crazy?" Kalina shouted as she raced around the next corner even as the walls shifted closer.

"You can do it, Kalina!" Luna hollered back as she raced across the top of the walls, their movement not causing a single hitch in her stride as she kept pace with Kalina, both of them racing toward the next target.

Kalina shut out all other distractions, including Zara, who appeared at the eighth target, and Luna, who kept leaping across the maze from one wall to the next, giggling madly the entire way.

The tenth target was the hardest. High in the sky, the dot almost invisible to the naked eye, Kalina still shot her arrow without hesitation and grinned in fierce joy when the walls shifted back to their original position.

"You did it, Kalina, you did it!" Luna leapt down from the walls to land next to Kalina and flung her arms around her.

"Congratulations, Kalina," Zara said as she landed next to her sister. "You're going to be amazing at the Trials."

Mitaru, who was lounging on a bench at the end of the maze, stood and grinned at the three of them. "Pretty impressive, Kalina. Less than twenty seconds between each target. Total time: three minutes and eighteen seconds. Incredible shooting and I'm especially grateful you didn't shoot my insane sister." He hooked around Luna's neck and dragged her close. "What were you thinking, crazy one?"

"That Kalina has to be ready for anything."

She was right. Kalina should have been able to

adjust and make that shot on the fly, even with Luna surprising her. She needed to do better.

"You're not thinking that you made a mistake, are you?" Zara demanded.

Luna pulled away from her brother and looked at Kalina. "Don't be silly, Kalina. You directed the shot away from the target to keep me safe. That's exactly what a Guardian would do. It's that kind of thing that will make you one of the best Guardians to ever serve in their ranks."

"She's right," Mitaru said. "I wouldn't be surprised if you're not heading your own unit within the year. To be clear, though, I expect to be part of that unit. Understood?"

Kalina grinned. "Absolutely!"

It wasn't until the last day before the trials that the four of them made it to the cochari hunting grounds, the only place on the infamous list they hadn't yet visited and the one place Kalina was truly excited about.

The cochari had the unique ability among all the animals in Faerie, to project a glamour much like the Fae did, masking their true form when hunting.

Kalina was really looking forward to seeing if she could pick out the cochari from their prey.

When they reached the hunting grounds, they chose

a couple boulders high above the grazing elk and deer and watched closely.

"There," Kalina said, pointing to one of the elk, who had slowly made its way toward the center of the field.

"Why him?" Zara asked.

"He's good, but he's clearly on a mission. Look at how he moves. He's not really grazing like the rest of them."

"There's another one." Mitaru pointed to the opposite side of the field. "He's edging toward that cluster of deer over there."

"Oh, I can't watch," Zara moaned.

For long moments, the cochari pretended to graze with their prey, still projecting the peaceful elegance of the elk and deer around them.

Then from one moment to the next, they exploded into their true forms, a rainbow of colors, red the brightest of them all, and one long horn they used to stab their prey. Then, of course, the flashing fangs as they attached themselves to the neck of their prey and bore them to the ground for feasting.

As weird as it might seem, Kalina found the hunt brought her as much peace as the hummingbirds, perhaps because it was all in the natural order of things.

Zara, however, wasn't so enthused. "Oh, no. I didn't really think this through, coming here," she fretted.

"Maybe I should help? You know, go down there and heal them?"

"Eh, I think they're a bit beyond healing," Mitaru said. "But you can practice on us." With that, he whirled on Kalina and though she leapt back, he still caught the edge of her upper arm, slashing a bright red line across it.

Kalina let out a hoot of laughter and drew her swords. "I call foul!" With that, she flung herself into the fight.

There, high above the cochari hunting grounds, the two of them pit their skills against one another again.

Even as the clang of their swords rang through the air, Kalina registered the sting and burn of Zara's healing power, closing the wound on her shoulder mere seconds after Mitaru had opened it.

She dodged and danced with him, a comforting sense of timelessness to the ritual, one they had indulged in thousands of times throughout the years.

As they fought, lines of red appeared and disappeared as first Zara, then Luna, healed them.

By the time they declared the fight a draw, twilight had fallen and the fields below were empty of both prey and predator.

CHAPTER 5

The Trials were divided into three phases.

The first phase—the Arena Trials— lasted seven days, five spent in combat with other Potentials and two spent resting and recovering.

The second phase—the Elemental Trials—took four days, three spent in the woods, demonstrating Fae mastery of the elements and of nature, and one again in rest and recovery.

The third phase, known only as the Final Trial, took place on the last day and was a complete mystery. Everyone's final trial was unique to them, and according to rumor, was the most challenging to pass.

In all, the Trials lasted twelve days and would become progressively more difficult as the days advanced.

The Arena Trials were intensely physical, as Thorne had expected, but also emotionally brutal in a way he had not.

He had not taken into account the fact that every win of his meant someone else went defeated and how much he would hate watching the dream of becoming a Guardian fade from his opponent's eyes as they clasped each other's arms in respect after a good bout.

It was easy in the beginning, but as he progressed through the first phase of the Trials, all of which took place in the Arena, it became harder. Harder because those he fought were better and more determined and believed more fiercely in their destiny to become a Guardian.

The battles were harder, the swordplay intense and fierce, the magic they called more and more dangerous and the injuries piled up.

There were healers on hand, of course, to heal any life-threatening injuries, but once a healer was called, disqualification followed.

Thorne couldn't wait for this phase to be over. He understood it was the quickest way to eliminate much of the competition, but he hated battling other Fae whose only crime was that they too wanted the honor of becoming a Guardian of the Veils.

By the time he left the arena on the fifth and final day of phase one, he was exhausted, covered in bruises and minor cuts, but full of relief. Rankings would be posted in the morning, but he was content in the knowledge that he'd made it at least into the top twenty, possibly even the top ten.

When he stepped out of the locker room, he found Tarek and Nako waiting. Nako had finished earlier in the day and had joined Tarek in the stands to watch the final bouts.

Thorne grinned at them both.

"You were amazing!" Tarek crowed. "Nako too. Did you see him?"

"I did. I'll be shocked if he doesn't make number one."

Nako just let out a grunt.

Thorne knew he was still annoyed that he'd almost lost the last bout against Jodahn, a Fae from a neighboring village, who was probably going to make it into the top ten. That battle had ultimately been declared a draw, but it had been close several times.

"Take heart, Nako," Thorne said. "If you're annoyed about Jodahn, imagine how he must feel. He couldn't beat a Fae three hundred years his junior."

Nako grinned. "Okay, there is that. Every time I get annoyed, I'm going to remember the look on his face when we clasped arms at the end of our bout."

"Annoyance?" Tarek guessed.

"Respect."

Thorne and Tarek made identical grunts of satisfaction, the sound so similar it may have come from the same person, causing all three of them to burst into laughter.

"Come on," Nako said. "I could really use a drink."

The first phase of the Trials went by in a flash, possibly because Kalina didn't find them to be that challenging. There were no combat situations she hadn't already practiced every month for the past four hundred years with Mitaru.

They had challenged each other as often and as best as they could and those practice bouts had prepared them both for the Arena Trials.

In the end, they left the Arena and the first phase of the Trials, confident they would at least progress to the second phase.

They celebrated with Luna and Zara, eating and dancing the hours away, with Kalina trying her best to relax and not worry about what was yet to come.

The next morning, they wandered into the hall where breakfast was being served to a hail of cheers and congratulations.

Kalina had landed the top slot in the first phase of

the Western Trials while Mitaru had landed the second.

Rumors flew that their scores were among the best of their generation, though no one could officially confirm scores from the other quadrants.

Kalina didn't care so much about the rankings as she did about simply placing and she was worried about the next two phases.

The Second Phase began with a challenge she wasn't sure they could win. They were divided into groups of twenty and taken to a clearing in the Goyavan Forest where they were told their only task was to save every single tree in the forest right before a fire broke out on all sides.

Chaos reigned as most of the Fae started conjuring water and dirt and anything else they could think of to stop the fire.

Mitaru and Kalina hung back and observed for a few moments.

"What do you think?" Mitaru asked.

"I think the fire is magical in nature. See how the water is doing nothing? It's almost like the water isn't there."

"Or the fire isn't."

Kalina thought about that for a moment. "But the trees are burning. I can hear them screaming."

"What kind of fire burns, but doesn't die? That isn't affected by water?"

"I don't know, but our task wasn't to put out the fire."

"Right. It was to save the trees."

"Earth magic," they said together.

They both dropped to their knees and dug their hands deep into the soil.

"Wake and hear me, I call upon thee," Kalina murmured softly.

"Wake and hear me, I call upon thee," Mitaru echoed.

"Wake and hear our call, we call upon the earth near and far," they chanted together. "Heal thyself. Heal these trees. Life we pour upon thee."

Around them, other Fae began to notice what they were doing and fell to their knees, buried their own hands in the soil and began to chant as well.

"Wake and hear our call, we call upon the earth near and far. Heal thyself. Heal these trees. Life we pour upon thee."

As the chanting grew and rose in volume, the ground beneath them began to glow, silvery strands of light streaking from where the Fae knelt, hands buried in the soil, to the trees engulfed in flames.

As the silver light traveled over the roots of the trees, the trees themselves began to glow, one after the other until the light from one tree leapt to the next and the next again until the entire Goyavan Forest was lit from the inside out, engulfed in the brilliant light of earth magic.

"This isn't working," Nako called to Thorne.

"I know, but what else can we do?" Thorne yelled back.

They stood surrounded by the ancient trees of Variona, all of them engulfed in flames, burning and screaming in pain.

"This had better be a bit of high-tech glamour," Nako yelled. "If these trees are suffering for our incompetence, I'll be right pissed off."

Thorne let out a huff of exasperation and let the water he had called to battle the fires dissipate.

"What are you doing?" Nako exclaimed, even as he dropped his hands and let the water he'd been redirecting from the rivers of Zajek flow back to their source.

"There has to be something we're missing." As he stared at the blaze, observing how it never moved toward the Fae, but also never seemed impacted by the spray of the waters, he was on the verge of remembering something or suggesting something when—

"Did you hear that?"

"What?"

"That song. It sounds like—of course." He spun to Nako. "Earth magic. Now."

The two fell to their knees and dug their hands deep into the earth and began to chant, a chant Thorne would swear he could already hear, from a voice both powerful and sweet.

"Wake and hear our call, we call upon the earth near and far." Thorne and Nako chanted. "Heal thyself. Heal these trees. Life we pour upon thee."

Around them, the other Fae fell to their knees and began to chant as well. In moments, the entire Woods of Variona were engulfed in light.

When the Fae walked out of the woods that afternoon, they were greeted with cheers and congratulations.

"How did you figure it out?" Nako asked Thorne when they were alone that night.

"I didn't. Not really. I heard someone chanting the Song of Earth Magic and I knew just what to do."

"I didn't hear anything."

"I'm telling you, I heard the song."

The next day, there were rumors that the Fae in the West had figured it out first and that their power had been so great, the Fae in the East had heard their chanting and joined in.

"There were trees near the end of their life cycles,"

one of the commanders in charge of the Trials was overheard saying to another. "They were ready to plunge to the earth. Those trees are now healthy and strong again, all because of the song of this generation's Potentials."

"It's what they do, Commander," the other man had said. "They heal and protect. It's in their nature."

"Yes, but they're not even Guardians yet. How powerful this generation must be to heal such a thing as old age."

"I heard it was just one Fae." Another commander spoke up. "One Fae who figured it out and led the rest."

"That's the way it usually is in these Trials," the first commander pointed out. "After all, leadership and teamwork are as important, perhaps even more so, than any of the powers these Fae may wield."

Centuries later, Thorne would think back to those two moments.

That moment in the woods when he heard her voice for the very first time—clear as a bell, strong in power, *enchanting*—and later, that moment when someone recounted the commanders' conversation about the song and the actions of one, the one Fae whose voice he'd heard and who would later turn out to be his fated mate.

CHAPTER 6

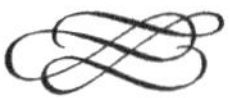

The second day in the woods wasn't anywhere near as fulfilling as the first.

Kalina had ended that first day filled with a true sense of purpose, exhilarated that she had finally had the opportunity to use her magic for a higher calling.

They had stopped a forest fire and saved some truly ancient trees.

She was fairly certain the trees hadn't been in any real danger. The Fae would never condone such willful destruction of an ancient forest, so she imagined the fire had been magically constructed.

It had felt real, though, and it had demonstrated to her the importance of the Guardians in this world, beyond just protecting the Veil.

They were servants, not just to the Veil, but to

Faerie itself and to all of its inhabitants, from the Fae to the trees to the beasts that wandered its lands.

So she was a little disappointed at how basic the second challenge in the woods was.

It was a standard hunt and race. The woods had been transformed into an obstacle course filled with traps and challenges, misdirections and clues that led them to the final task, which, to Kalina's disgust, ended up being the rescue of a Fae princess.

Kalina knew it was a princess because she had the marks of the throne across her face and hands, and also because there was an entire regimen of Royal Guardians surrounding the cell and one fierce looking Guardian standing inside it between the door and the princess.

Kalina was fairly certain, based on the blue hair, that this was Princess Astra. If she had eyes to match, Kalina would know for certain, but at the moment, she couldn't tell because the princess was sitting on a bench, calmly reading a book.

Kalina let out a huge sigh. "Seriously? They couldn't have imprisoned a prince instead?"

Astra looked up from her book and grinned.

Kalina inhaled at the sight of her dark blue eyes. They really did match her hair.

"Oh, don't worry." Astra stood and placed a leaf inside the book, marking her place. "They sent my two brothers to the North and the South." She stood and walked across the cell toward Kalina. "My oldest brother, though, refused to participate. Glory, who was sent to the East, and I have decided we'll be getting even somehow. He knows it though, so we'll be waiting a bit, just to be sure his guard is down."

The Guardian at Astra's side smiled a little, amusement and affection in his eyes as he glanced down at her.

It didn't make him any less scary or intimidating.

"I suppose that's all right then," Kalina said. "As long as we're not pandering to those idiotic cliches about Fae princesses needing rescuing."

Astra giggled. "Absolutely no cliches over here." She leaned forward and whispered, rather loudly, "But don't tell my Guardians. They like to think they're indispensable."

"Your secret's safe with me," Kalina said dryly. "So, what am I supposed to do now? Do you need me to break you out of there?"

"Oh, yes, I'm afraid they've spelled the bars and the key lock. Oh, you really shouldn't touch it because—" She broke off as the lock Kalina was tinkering with unlatched and fell to the floor.

"All right then, I guess you're free, Princess Astra." Kalina pushed open the cell door and grinned at her stunned expression.

"How did you do that? No one's ever done that. Not ever, have they, Kahji?"

"Never." The Guardian at Astra's side glared at Kalina suspiciously.

Kalina grinned. "Mitaru and I spent our third century perfecting our air magic. We've learned how to use it specifically for opening locks and getting out of chains. To be honest, this lock wasn't very much of a challenge at all."

"I've never even considered using air magic for such a task," Kahji said. "That's ingenious."

"Why, thank you. It was actually Mitaru's idea."

"And who is this Mitaru?" Astra asked.

"Mitaru Verushi, at your service." Mitaru stepped up to Kalina's side and swept a bow toward the princess, who giggled and curtsied in return.

Kahji scowled at Mitaru, then swung Astra around to his other side, so that he stood between them.

Interesting.

The princess seemed oblivious as to why she'd been moved, but it was pretty clear to Kalina.

She grinned at Mitaru. "About time you got here."

Mitaru rolled his eyes. "I'm not as swift as you in the trees, you know that. I'm pretty sure no one is. In fact, I begin to question whether you cheat and sprout wings."

"Huh. I never considered trying that."

"I wouldn't suggest it," Kahji said. "I only know of

one idiot who actually tried to fly and the results were not pretty. Anyway, you'd better get on with it, young man."

He waved a hand and the door to the cell clanged shut and the lock that had been on the ground flew back into place, locking Kahji and the princess once again behind bars.

"Oh, right." Mitaru stepped forward and in less time than it had taken Kalina, sent an arrow of air into the lock mechanism and jiggled it, causing the lock to spring open and fall to the floor.

This time, Kalina noticed, Kahji watched the entire process closely and she knew he'd be practicing with locks and air magic before the night was out.

"That was fun," Mitaru said as they left the cave where they'd found the princess. "I wouldn't be surprised if she doesn't ask you to join her Royal Guard. She was most impressed with how quickly you arrived, not to mention the lock trick, though I think Guardian Kahji was even more intrigued."

"Then they should invite you. After all, you're the one who came up with the idea and you're ever so much faster at it than I am."

"Eh. I'm for the Veils, you know that."

Kalina grinned. "As am I."

The second day of Phase Two, they were sent into the woods in groups of twenty with the admonishment that they were not allowed to work together, that they were being timed and that they had exactly eight hours to solve the quest and capture their prize.

Thorne entered the cave with a smirk.

He wasn't in first place, mostly because he'd had too much fun trailing Nako and Jodahn, who were clearly pitting their every skill against each other. The last he'd seen of them, they'd been racing through the upper story of the trees like a pair of crazed monkeys. He lost sight of them about a mile back and was pretty certain they would have beaten him here.

"So are you our prize?"

Thorne raised an eyebrow. That was Nako's voice and it sounded like he was flirting.

"Princesses are not prizes." The haughty voice made Thorne grin.

Shot down.

Not that Nako would mind.

Thorne would bet he was flirting just to get Jodahn all hot and bothered.

"Come on now. They told us not to leave the forest

without our prize and here you are. She looks like a prize, doesn't she, Jodahn?"

Thorne rounded a corner in the cave and took in the scene in front of him.

A young woman stood behind some bars in a cell. There were two Guardians at her back and a number of other Guardians stationed throughout the chamber.

Thorne was guessing this was Princess Glory based on the purple hair and eyes, not to mention the markings of the throne that marched across her face.

Jodahn stood off to the side, arms crossed, scowl on his face as Nako faced the woman through the bars and flirted.

Thorne rolled his eyes and strode forward. He slung an arm around Nako's shoulders and said to the Princess, "Never mind this one. He's just being an ass, probably attracted to Jodahn over there." He raised an eyebrow at the princess. "Or possibly the guards at your side."

Nako let out a low growl, slammed his elbow into Thorne's side, jerked free and growled, "Always ruining my fun, aren't you? Okay, then, Princess Glory. If you're not the prize, what is?"

"You don't get the prize until you've broken me out of here. And you three cannot work together, so two of you will have to step around the corner and wait your turn."

Thorne straightened and said, "Well, as I was definitely in third place, I'll step out. Hurry up then, won't you?"

A moment after he stepped around the corner, Nako joined him.

Thorne raised an eyebrow. "Jodahn beat you?"

"The man's fast. Too bad he's going to make it into the Guard with us."

"I knew it. You're attracted."

"Of course, I am. Have you seen him?"

Thorne shrugged. He was indifferent to men, for the most part. Women, however…

"Who's next?"

"I guess that's me. Wish me luck." Nako grinned and sauntered away.

A few moments later, the same Guardian who had come for Nako returned and gestured Thorne in.

It took Thorne almost the entirety of the five minutes he was given to release the lock.

He got shocked almost immediately.

Bad magic there, but a mix of earth and fire spells eventually dissipated the spell protecting the lock mechanism and he managed to pick it in record time.

"Nicely done. The two before you may have been faster, but they're not thieves at heart." Princess Glory passed him a tiny strip of cloth. It was white and had etched in one corner the number three and on the opposite corner a tiny opened lock. "Your prize. Now run along as there are more Potentials coming."

Thorne grinned and bowed low to show his respect for the throne. "Thank you, Princess Glory. A thousand blessings."

Outside the cave, he found Nako and Jodahn waiting.

"You got the prize!" Nako scowled.

"You didn't?"

"I couldn't get the lock open."

"Nor could I," Jodahn grumbled.

"So, what now? They said not to leave without it."

"Well, as far as I'm concerned, you have it and we're with you," Nako said.

Thorne gave a snort of amusement. "Fine, but don't blame me if you get disqualified."

"Trust me. I know it didn't seem difficult to you, but that lock was impossible. Most of the Fae here will fail just like we did."

As it turned out, Nako was right, and when a Fae was unable to open the lock, they did exactly what Nako and Jodahn did. They waited outside the cave until someone who succeeded came out with the prize. Then, they all walked out of the woods together.

"What do you think will happen if the last person in doesn't open the lock?" Nako mused as they watched yet another group file into the arena and settle in the stands to wait with everyone else. "There won't be anyone after them to win the prize."

"Well, first of all, they'll probably be disqualified by virtue of being the last one in," Jodahn said.

"Maybe, but just because they're last in their group doesn't mean they're the last overall. Besides, what if they end up wandering through the woods forever?"

"I doubt the princess would allow that to happen," Thorne said. His words proved prophetic as a few moments later, the Princess and her Guardians entered the arena, with the final group of candidates.

A few moments later, the rankings went live, scrolling across the floor of the arena.

Thorne was surprised to see his own name listed first. "But I got there after you two."

"Yeah, but we didn't open the lock. You did. That gave you enough points to vault you to first," Nako said. "Nice job."

"You too. Look at you in third place."

Nako sent a mock glare over at Jodahn, who just raised an eyebrow in response. "It's the brute's fault. He tripped a trap, only it caught me instead of him."

"Need to be faster than the traps," Jodahn said with a smirk.

On the third day of the second phase, Kalina reported to the arena to discover they were being divided into groups of ten. Their numbers appeared to have been greatly reduced since the day before, perhaps by as much as fifty percent.

She didn't know anyone in the group she was assigned, but wasn't nervous until Mitaru's group returned and all of them, including Mitaru, looked spooked.

He stared down at his feet as he moved to the opposite side of the arena, where those who had already finished the day's Trial were gathered.

She had a feeling he wasn't looking in her direction to keep her from seeing the distress in his eyes.

It didn't matter though because she could see it

every line of his body, in the way he moved and in the slump of his shoulders.

And just like that, all the nerves that had disappeared after winning her first bout in the Arena Trials came roaring back.

They didn't lessen as the day wore on and more and more groups left and returned and the sounds in the arena became more and more subdued.

It was late afternoon and the crowds had dwindled until only Kalina and her group were seated in their section, when they were finally called.

They were led out of the arena and down a path toward the woods. Right before they would have entered the woods, their guide veered to the left and walked them along the edge of the woods until a new pathway appeared.

As they entered the woods, they met the group that had been called right before them. They each filed passed silently, the same subdued look on their faces.

Once the group had passed, their guide led them further into the woods and down a steep winding path.

About fifteen minutes later, they exited the woods again and found themselves in a large clearing with the woods at their back and if she wasn't mistaken, a very tiny veil in front of them.

They were nowhere near the official borders where

the Guardians served and yet, there it was: a tiny pocket in space.

A roaming Veil.

She'd never seen one before, but she knew they existed.

Most Fae hoped never to encounter one.

A roaming Veil could appear anywhere at anytime and they were a magnet for the Sorenalaya.

The Fae had many tales and songs of the Sorenalaya, the Fae who had faded so far from this world, they were reduced to the insubstantial forms of their beasts. So thin as to be almost transparent, with claws and fangs, they craved human flesh and souls, and so roamed the borderlands, constantly testing the Veils in the hope to cross over and feast upon the mortal worlds.

It was a Guardian's job to stop them.

It was why the majority of Guardians served close to the Veils, so that they could monitor and strengthen the Veils when they weakened and drive back the Sorenalaya.

"I see some of you recognize what we have here," Commander Tanier spoke quietly, but the sound of his voice brought stillness to the Fae as everyone turned to listen. "As Guardians, your job will sometimes involve traveling days on end to reach one of these isolated, weakened portions of the Veil. You may arrive exhausted and wish for nothing more than a good night's sleep, but the mortals the Sorenalaya prey upon will not thank you for your hesitation.

"Even when exhausted, covered in mud from a weeklong journey across brutal terrain, you will be expected to battle any Sorenalaya still lingering around the Veil *and* to pursue any that managed to cross into the mortal realms. In other words, to sum up." He ticked off each point with his fingers. "Battle-ready. Healing magic and a strong life force to strengthen the veil. Glamour to shield your true form from the mortals. Tracking abilities to find the Sorenalaya. And compassion to offer them peace as swiftly as possible. These are the bare minimum qualities required of a Guardian, regardless of how exhausted or weary or even injured that Guardian may be.

"This will be your duty, day in and day out as a Guardian of the Veil. And your reward for a thousand years of service to this duty shall be death. You will throw yourselves upon the Veil, surrender your physical forms and burn your life force to ash for the good of all the Fae.

"This is the lot of a Guardian of the Veil. If you were hoping to become a Royal Guardian, that honor is only ever offered to a Guardian after many centuries of service to the Veil and it is a rare Guardian, indeed, who is chosen. If that is your hope, you should leave the Trials now." He waited.

A few of the Fae shifted their feet uneasily, but no one left the clearing.

"Very well then. Today, you will discover whether you have what it takes to become a Guardian of the Veil in truth. This portion of the Veil has been guarded since it was discovered. No Sorenalaya have been allowed to use it for entrance to the mortal realms. You ten will work together to ensure this continues to be true.

"I'll be observing from that tree there." He gestured toward a tree at the edge of the woods. "Your task is to defend the Veil at all costs against any Sorenalaya who come near, and believe me, they will come.

"Do not hesitate, Fae, for hesitation will result at the very least, in the loss of mortal lives, and at the very most, in the loss of your own souls. Be vigilant, Fae, and protect the Veil."

"We need a plan," Kalina said the minute the Commander left them to walk toward the tree he had chosen.

The other Fae turned to her. They looked as nervous as she felt and they hadn't even seen a Sorenalaya yet.

The Sorenalaya had lost their connection to life and to nature. To defeat them, the Fae had to fill their forms with both.

It required a delicate balance of both life and earth

magic, but first a Sorenalaya had to be contained and the best way to do that was through fire magic.

"Who has the strongest fire magic among us?"

"I'm pretty strong," a male Fae with bright green eyes and hair said.

"I am too," a female said.

"Okay, you two need to be by the Veil. Surround it in fire. Everyone else—"

"Sorenalaya!" one of the Fae cried out.

"Fire magic," Kalina shouted. "Defend the Veil and ring them in fire, Fae!"

As the Fae scrambled into position, forming a loose circle around the tiny pocket in space, Kalina caught her first glimpse of the Sorenalaya.

There was nothing that even remotely resembled the Fae in their appearance. They were all fangs and claws and a terrible screeching sound as they rushed toward them.

"Earth magic," Thorne shouted as they faced off against the Sorenalaya.

He called roots from the earth as quickly as possible, causing them to explode from the ground, where they writhed through the insubstantial forms of the Sorenalaya.

Still the Sorenalaya fought on, breaking free of the roots to attack again and again.

The Fae slowed them down with more and more earth magic, roots exploding everywhere, but it wasn't enough.

The Sorenalaya continually broke free and fought on, desperate to reach the Veil.

They would need more than just earth magic to win this battle.

Digging deep for a tiny drop of his own life force, Thorne sent a coil of life magic down his swords, infusing the blades with its power.

He swung them at the closest Sorenalaya. It was so insubstantial, he wasn't certain his blades, even glowing with life magic, would have an effect, but the Sorenalaya exploded, ash cascading everywhere, floating on the wind.

Thorne leapt to the next Sorenalaya and shouted, "Infuse your blades with life magic, Guardians!"

Kalina wasn't sure how other Fae conjured fire, but she simply envisioned a tiny sun sitting in the palm of her hand and then hurtled it upward, closing her hand at the very last second, catching the tail end of the fire rope she'd shaped from that tiny sun. Arm up, she whirled the fire rope round and round so that it crackled and snapped in the air above her.

All around her, the other Fae were conjuring their own fire lassos and as one, they snapped their hands out.

Kalina's rope met the ropes of two others and they formed a giant lasso that fell around two of the Sorenalaya, becoming a ring of fire that surrounded them.

Though the Sorenalaya were insubstantial and could not be harmed by fire, for reasons no one quite understood, they were terrified of the flames and would often freeze when faced with fire, perhaps simply an instinctive remnant of their long-forgotten physical lives.

A quick glance showed her that the Fae had managed to ring all of the Sorenalaya in fire, so she focused on the next step. She imagined roots sprouting from the souls of her feet, digging deep and spreading through the lands.

She then envisioned the earth pouring its energy through those roots in and out, over and over again, until they were quivering with life.

When they were ready, they moved toward the ring of fire that surrounded the Sorenalaya.

She became aware as her roots expanded through the soil that there were roots moving on either side of her, the earth magic of the two Fae whose lassoes had joined hers.

The roots met beneath the ring of fire, right at its center, and exploded from beneath, twining around and through the Sorenalaya frozen inside.

Kalina tried to ignore the shrieking of the Sorenalaya, just as she tried not to think about how this had been the fate of—

One of the Sorenalaya let out a shriek and leapt forward, breaking free of the roots and hurtling past the barrier of fire. It caught the Fae to Kalina's left in its grasp and with a shrieking wail began to suck the Fae's life force from him.

For a moment, Kalina was frozen, then she heard as if from a great distance, "Infuse your blades with life magic, Guardians!" and grabbed her dagger.

She wrenched free a tiny drop of her life force, twined it around a strand of magic, and poured both over the blade. She then plunged the dagger through the Sorenalaya, right where its heart should be.

For a terrible moment in time, she thought it hadn't worked, but then the Sorenalaya fell back away from the Fae it had been feeding upon and on its way down, morphed for one split second back to the Fae Kalina imagined it had once been, then was gone in a shower of ash.

The Fae fell to his knees and coughed out his thanks.

The rest of their group was in a standoff with the Sorenalaya. The fire was enough to keep most of them pinned and the earth magic had them wailing in pain, but they weren't dying.

"How did you do that?" The Fae on the ground wheezed.

"Our swords aren't working on them," a Fae from across the way called.

"They're too insubstantial," a third yelled.

"Infuse your blades with life magic," Kalina called back as she decapitated another Sorenalaya.

"I didn't even know you could do that," the Fae she'd saved called to her as he rejoined the battle to give peace to the Sorenalaya.

Neither had she, at least not until she'd heard that voice.

Later, when they had dispatched the last of the Sorenalaya, she questioned the other Guardians in the clearing and the Commander who had watched from the trees, but none of them admitted to being the one she'd heard.

They all believed it was her intuition telling her what to do, but Kalina knew the truth.

She'd heard a voice—strong, male, compelling—and she'd done exactly what he'd ordered without thought, without hesitation, and in the process had saved a Fae's life and given peace to the Sorenalaya.

"Well, that was just horrible," Nako said.

Thorne had to agree.

No matter how he'd prepared for the possibility of becoming a Guardian and no matter how many accounts he'd read of Fae Guardians defending the mortal worlds against the Sorenalaya, nothing could have prepared him for what they had just seen and done.

Knowing they were once Fae made it all the worse.

The Sorenalaya were more terrifying than he'd realized and he'd thought them pretty horrifically terrifying before.

Now he knew exactly what the future looked like for the Faded and he made a pledge then and there to never fade from this world, no matter how bleak his life became.

Then again, he was closer than he'd ever been to achieving his dream of becoming a Guardian of the Veil, and if that happened, he would never have to worry about fading, for he would sacrifice himself upon the Veils long before old age had him ever contemplating a fade.

If old age did not drag a Fae into the fade, the only other thing that could, was the loss of a mate. More often than not, though, mates went into their eternity together.

Not that Thorne had to worry about that eventuality either since no Guardian of the Veil had ever found a fated mate.

"I wasn't sure my group was going to survive for a minute there," Nako said.

"I'm pretty sure that was the point," Thorne said.

"What do you mean?"

"That whole Trial was a demonstration of what we'll be facing as Guardians of the Veil. I'd be willing to bet there are any number of Potentials packing their bags right now."

Nako groaned. "Can you imagine? Getting this far and then giving up?"

"Better to give up now than discover too late you're not cut out for the job. It would be a thousand times worse to die in your first battle with the Sorenalaya."

"True."

"Besides, those who show up for tomorrow's Trial will be truly dedicated and believe this is their calling."

"Well, that's definitely me," Nako said. "Because while it *was* rather terrifying, it was also an awesomely powerful adrenaline rush."

Thorne gave a snort of laughter. "Couldn't have said it better myself."

Rumors swept through the Trials that only two groups had been able to dispatch the Sorenalaya without help from the Commanders observing.

Other groups managed to trap the Sorenalaya or drive them back, but none had managed to give them peace.

This was the lesson every Guardian learned that day: to fight the Sorenalaya required more than one skill set. They had to be gifted in both earth magic *and* life magic and agility with blades and fire magic was a bonus that could save lives.

More importantly, to give peace to the Sorenalaya, to ensure they did not suffer needlessly, a Guardian had to be able to think under pressure and pull on any of those skills effortlessly and at a moment's notice.

Kalina was still pondering those lessons that evening at dinner when Mitaru joined her.

"I heard you made history today," he said.

"What are you talking about?"

"I overheard the commanders talking. Commander

Yarina said in thousands of years of Trial history, not one group of Fae has ever managed to dispatch peace to the Sorenalaya. It requires years of training."

"That doesn't even make sense. Why would they set us up for failure?"

"It makes perfect sense. It's a huge part of the job. We have to understand viscerally how difficult fighting the Sorenalaya really is. Think about it. I bet a hundred Fae, *at least*, are packing their bags right now, unwilling to spend their lives in battle with the Faded."

"I suppose." What a depressing thought, though.

"One of the Commanders said he'd never even considered infusing life magic into his blade before. He'd never tried it."

"I hadn't really considered it either, not until—"

"Until what?"

Kalina shook her head. "It doesn't matter. I might be going crazy."

Mitaru let out a snort of laughter.

"So how do they usually fight the Sorenalaya if they don't use their blades?"

"I guess they just throw the magic at them."

"That seems rather wasteful. What if the Sorenalaya move or the Fae's aim is off? So much magic would be lost if it wasn't contained somewhere."

"Yeah, that was the commander's point. He said it was ingenious and an excellent way to conserve one's power, and he was shocked none of them had ever considered doing it. That's why the commanders are so impressed. You know what Commander Yarina said about you and the Fae from the Eastern Trials?"

"What?"

"He said you two were the best candidates he'd ever seen, that you were truly something special."

Kalina shook her head. "But it wasn't me."

"What do you mean?"

"It wasn't my idea. I heard a voice, a Fae. I think it was him."

"Who?"

"Did they say who the other Fae was? The one in the Eastern Trials?"

"No. For all I know, it was a female."

"No. I heard his voice, commanding the Guardians to infuse their blades with life magic. I heard him and that's how I knew what to do."

"That doesn't even make sense. How could you hear a Fae halfway across the world?"

"I don't know, but I did."

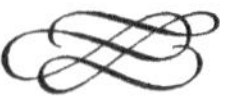

CHAPTER 8

"What do you think the Final Trial will be?" Luna asked at lunch the next day.

"I have no idea," Kalina said. "All I know is everyone's Trial is different."

"That seems pretty time-consuming," Zara said.

"Not if they use magic," Kalina said. "I'm just not sure how they would manage it."

"My guess is a fear spell," Mitaru said. "They're not that difficult to build or maintain so they can work on any number of people at the same time."

"Well, what's your worst fear?" Luna asked.

"Losing you two," Mitaru said.

"Aw," Luna and Zara chorused together.

"What about you, Kalina?" Zara asked.

Kalina shrugged. "Honestly, I have no idea. I don't really think about fears that much."

"Well, my guess is you'll know what it is by the end of the day tomorrow," Mitaru said.

"Great."

Thorne left the arena feeling sick. If anyone had told him what he would face in the Final Trial, he may not have signed up.

"Are you okay? Hey, Thorne." Tarek stepped into his path and put a hand on his shoulder. "Brother, what's wrong? You look like you've seen a ghost."

Thorne didn't answer, just stepped forward and dragged his younger brother into his arms for a tight hug before shoving him back again. "I'm fine now." He cleared his throat. "Everything's fine now. Where's Nako?"

"He's in the locker room puking his insides out. I guess the Final Trial was epically bad, huh?"

"You could say that."

*K*alina found herself standing in a cottage with no memory of how she'd gotten there.

The sound of a baby crying got louder and a gorgeous male Fae stepped into the outer room where she stood. He had beautiful dark skin and brilliant green eyes.

In his arms was a baby, who had the same dark skin and green eyes. She stopped crying the moment she saw Kalina and stretched forward, arms out. "Mama!"

Kalina's entire world shuddered.

This couldn't be happening.

"Mama!"

"She's been crying for you. Are you sure you really want to sacrifice yourself upon the Veils?" The Fae stared at her hard. His voice was so familiar. Where had she heard that voice? "Are you really going to leave her alone like your mother left you?"

Kalina wanted to scream that this could not be the life she had chosen for herself, not when she had spent her childhood vowing to adhere to the truth of what it meant to be a Guardian.

She had grown up hearing the stories of her terribly selfish mother, Sefina, who had wanted both the honor of being a Guardian *and* to leave something physical of herself behind.

It was expected of all Guardians that when they shed their physical forms in service to the Veils of Faerie, that all that would be left of them in this world was the memory of their strength and sacrifice.

Yet, Sefina had defied tradition to court and win a Fae who was not her mate. She had then gone so far as to create an infant with that male, something that should have been impossible, then left the child alone in his care as she went back to her destiny.

And so, Kalina had grown up without a mother. Without a father too, for despite not being mates, her father had Faded in the aftermath of her mother's death.

Staring at the child, remembering her vow never to follow in her mother's footsteps, the truth of who she was began to splinter the reality around her.

"Well, Kalina?" the Fae demanded, his voice somehow wrong, a note of anger that didn't belong. "Will you abandon your mate and your child as your mother abandoned your father and you?"

"No," Kalina said. "I will not because I will not have a mate or child to abandon." She turned and walked out of the cottage.

The moment she stepped over the threshold, reality fractured again and she found herself standing in the arena.

She glanced at the clock projected high above the

floor and saw she'd only been in the Trial for three minutes, twenty-seven seconds.

Whispers exploded throughout the stands.

 itaru kept asking how she'd broken through the glamour so quickly, but Kalina wasn't sure how to answer.

Mitaru had been completely accurate about his greatest fear and he'd come out of the Final Trial nauseous and vomiting because it had forced him to choose between saving his sisters and saving the Veils.

To his horror, in that dream realm, he had chosen the Veils.

"It wasn't real, Mitaru!"

"But I didn't know that, Kalina. It felt so real. I truly believed I was a Guardian and that the Veils were in danger of falling and that the only way to save them was to sacrifice Luna and Zara *and I did it.*"

"You'll never have to make that choice, Mitaru, and if you do, I know you'll find a different way to save Faerie and your sisters. Nothing could convince me that you would sacrifice them instead."

"But I *did.*"

The worst part for Mitaru was that in failing his

sisters, he also gained entrance to the Guardian Force. It left him weighted down with guilt and cast a shadow upon the inauguration ceremonies that followed.

A moment that should have been one of triumph had a solemnity and sorrow to it that Kalina had difficulty understanding.

She'd walked out of the Trials, feeling stronger in her belief that she was meant for this path. By contrast, most of her fellow Guardians looked slightly ill, as if they were even then, in the very moment of their inauguration, doubting they were on the right path.

When her name was called, immediately after Mitaru's, she stepped forward and Commander Yarina pinned the symbol of the Guardians to her new uniform. "You broke a number of records in the Trials. I expect great things from you, Guardian Wyendeh."

"Yes, sir."

The rankings had been announced the day before and Kalina shared the top spot with a Guardian from the east named Thorne Evaria.

A name she'd whispered in her sleep the night before, waking her and making her wonder why that name sparked something deep inside.

As she pondered the mystery of that name, Commander Yarina continued down the line, pinning the symbol of the Guardian Fae to the uniforms of all those present.

Finally, it was time to repeat the vow of the Guardian Force, a moment Kalina had waited for her entire life.

The room echoed with the sound of one hundred twenty-five Fae pledging their lives to the Veils.

"We stand for the Fae and for all of Faerie. We pledge our life in service to the Veils and our life force as its last defense. We are Guardians of the Veil."

Kalina repeated the vow with an overwhelming sense of finally becoming the Fae she was always meant to be.

Mitaru, on the other hand, later told her he'd felt cold upon repeating that vow, as if he'd just severed his link to both Luna and Zara, leaving them to make their way in the world without their older brother at their side.

They had lost their parents long before, the two ancients succumbing to the lure of a final rest, leaving the three of them as the last of an ancient line of Fae.

Despite this, Mitaru had felt compelled to pledge his service to the Veils. It was something he'd longed for as Kalina had, from a very young age, and like Kalina, believed the mark of the Guardian that appeared on his face centuries before was proof that he was on the right path.

He took comfort in knowing Luna and Zara would have each other, but it wasn't enough to alleviate his guilt, especially after his experiences in the Final Trial.

Mitaru had come out of that Trial broken in a way that Kalina had not. Somehow, though, he took all those jagged pieces of his soul and he used them to become a better Guardian.

He obsessed over those moments, revisiting them, analyzing them, questioning what he should have done differently.

He was continually inventing scenarios for them to solve, where the task was both to save the Veils and to protect innocents like his sisters.

In a way, the Final Trial gave him the determination to never simply accept what was presumed to be true, but to instead explore beyond what was already known to see the endless possibilities at hand.

It also made him question *everything*. Why were Guardians destined to burn? Why did the Veils fail every five hundred years? What might they do differently to change the destiny of future Guardians and of Faerie itself?

Kalina indulged him and ran through scenarios with him, explored the possibilities, researched what was known about the Veils and what was unknown, but not once in any of those years did she question her purpose.

Instead, she accepted.

She accepted what she had lost in stepping forward into the role of Guardian.

She often dreamed of the Fae and the child in his arms, both of them reaching out, the male demanding that she face what she was giving up and the child simply crying, "Mama."

Kalina had never wanted children and thus, didn't really mourn the child for she was never going to exist, not even if Kalina had chosen another path in life. Therefore, she could look at the child and feel nothing but a sense of relief that this child would never, *could* never be hers.

When she looked at the man, though, that was when she understood what she had lost.

This was what she had given up to become a Guardian.

The possibility of one day finding her fated mate.

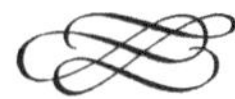

CHAPTER 9

Thorne loved being a Guardian.

It was even better now that Tarek had joined the ranks a hundred years before. Now he and his brother served together, though in different generations.

As Nako had jokingly promised all those years before, when it came time for them to mentor and partner with one of the incoming Guardians, he chose Tarek.

Though Tarek had rolled his eyes and acted as if it was a huge sacrifice to accept Nako as his mentor, Thorne could tell he was pleased.

At the same time Tarek and his generation were accepted into the ranks as Guardians, the generation before Nako and Thorne walked into their destinies, infusing their life force into the Veils of the East, for the good of all the Fae.

It was a difficult time for both Nako and Thorne, saying goodbye to their mentors, stepping up as mentors themselves and looking ahead, knowing they were on the downward slope toward their own destinies.

For this reason, Thorne was incredibly grateful to Nako. Though he would have been honored to accept Tarek as his mentee, by not doing so, he was able to enjoy his time with Tarek as simply brothers, a gift he cherished more and more as their time grew shorter.

Thorne had always believed his destiny was at the Eastern gates, serving as a Guardian of the Veil for the good of all the Fae. He'd been so at peace with that decision that before the Trials, he'd never spent a single sleepless night worrying about the future.

That changed from almost the very moment he began his tenure as a Guardian. His dreams were now haunted by a song he could never quite remember that filled him with sorrow and a terrible sense of loss.

Added to the weight of those dreams was the knowledge he would soon be leaving Tarek behind.

It would have been different if they had been able to serve in the same generation, but knowing that Tarek would be facing his fate without his brother at his side left scars on Thorne's soul.

He questioned whether he had made the right decision, not for himself, not even for the Fae, but for the
brother he loved more than life itself.

Then, as if things were not difficult enough, Fate
brought yet another challenge his way.

He traveled to the capital city of Eonara to attend a
fifteen-day training along with Guardians from all over
Faerie.

They were housed with the Guardians of the North
and trained with them, pitting their skills against other
units in intense training sessions.

Though Thorne knew there were Guardians from
the West and South training in the facilities as well, he
didn't meet any of them until the end of the first week,
when they had two days off to rest and to explore
Eonara before the second week of training began.

It was then, on their eighth day in Eonara that
Thorne met Kalina for the first time.

*K*alina loved being a Guardian. She had
found her family at last and it wasn't
the one she'd been born to.

Her aunt Madora had never forgiven her for
choosing the Guardians.

"Your mother was selfish and your father weak," Madora had snarled when Kalina returned from submitting her name to the Courts, "but I took you in despite all their failures. And this is how you repay me, by making the same choices your mother did?"

Madora had done nothing to hide her anger at her sister for the decisions she had made or her contempt for Kalina's father and his weak nature.

That anger and contempt had spilled over onto Kalina more times than she could count. The final blow had come when she submitted her name to be a Guardian in the same way her mother had. That act had broken something between aunt and niece that had never grown strong in the first place.

That broken bond grew increasingly frail and the day Kalina became a Guardian in truth, it withered to nothing.

Kalina had entered the Guardians alone, no family behind her giving her strength, and yet after six hundred years of serving with her fellow Guardians, she felt more empowered, more supported than ever before.

She had an entire generation of Guardians at her back and her best friend, Mitaru, to walk with her into their destiny.

She regretted nothing, not even the loss of that green-eyed mate she would never meet and who probably didn't even exist in this world, and she felt no sense of sorrow as their destiny approached, even though it meant leaving many behind, including Mitaru's sisters.

She knew he struggled more, and had since they'd reached the halfway mark a hundred years before.

As they began their descent into the last half of their service, it was clear the impending loss was beginning to weigh heavily upon Luna and Zara, which weighed heavily on Mitaru.

Kalina, however, had no regrets.

She would walk into her destiny knowing she did so to protect Luna and Zara and countless other Fae.

Mitaru had been right when he predicted she would lead a unit of her own one day. She had twenty-four Guardians in her unit and Mitaru was one of them.

As part of her job as their leader, Kalina was always looking for new training opportunities for her unit. This was how they ended up in Eonara, training with Guardians from the South one week and Guardians from the North the next.

The first week was intense and brutal and by the end of it, they were all ready for some relaxation time.

Most of the unit scattered, heading into different directions, some of them to meet up with friends or family and others to explore the city.

As was usual for their downtime, Kalina and Mitaru ended up spending much of it together.

"Your sisters couldn't join us for the weekend this time?" Kalina asked as she opened the door to the tavern they'd chosen for dinner.

"They're traveling again. You know how they love to visit the animals and gardens of the mortal realms."

"One of these days, they're going to get in trouble, you know." Kalina led the way toward a corner table at the back where they would both be able to sit with their backs to the wall.

She waited until they were both seated at the table before continuing. "Eventually some enterprising human will record them healing a feral cat or snuggling up to a giant bear and the Fae will be unveiled to billions of mortals all at once. There's no way we could manage that much magic and glamour to make an entire world forget our existence."

Mitaru snorted. "Wouldn't that be something? I'd be blessed with the opportunity to say to my sisters until the end of our days, 'I told you so.' Now you've got me almost wishing it would happen."

Kalina laughed.

"It's true. I've been saying for years that Lunastaria will be the downfall of us all."

"Well, let's hope it doesn't happen because—" Kalina's words died in her throat.

Three male Fae had just entered the Tavern. They were beautiful men, as were all the Fae, but Kalina only had eyes for the one in the middle.

Tall, dark skin, piercing green eyes.

"Kalina?"

"Sorry, I—" She looked away, but couldn't resist and glanced back again. The men headed to the bar, where they ordered drinks then walked to a table not too far from where she and Mitaru sat.

"What's wrong?" Mitaru straightened in his seat and followed Kalina's gaze. "Do you know them?"

"The one with the green eyes. I mean, I don't know him, but—"

Mitaru swung his head back toward Kalina. "Don't tell me that's your Dream Fae."

Kalina rolled her eyes. "I don't know, but we should go."

"We haven't even ordered."

"Mitaru, I can't—if that's him, I—"

"If that's him, you need to know."

Kalina shook her head. "What am I thinking? Of course, it's not him. I mean, maybe it is him, but it's not like we're Fated Mates. Guardians don't get mates, everybody knows that."

"Why not?"

"What do you mean why not?"

"I mean why does everyone claim we don't get

mates? How do they even know that?"

"Because it's never happened before?"

"What about your mother?"

Kalina scowled. "What about her?"

"How did she have you if your father wasn't her fated mate?"

"I don't know. Everyone says they weren't mates though. My aunt told me it was an aberration, that my mother must have used dark magic to quicken her womb for a man who wasn't her mate."

"That doesn't even make sense. If that were the case, then he would never have Faded in response to her death. You know it's true, Kalina. You may avoid thinking about it, but we all know it's true. There's no other explanation. They had to be mates."

"But that would mean it isn't true, about Guardians not having fated mates."

"Exactly."

"Why would they lie to us?"

"Leaving aside your own feelings about mates and being a Guardian, what do you think most Guardians would do if they met their mate and he or she wasn't a Guardian too?"

Kalina shook her head.

"Most Guardians would never make the choice your mother did. They would never leave their mate behind, to Fade from this world, to become Sorenalaya like your father."

Kalina blanched. She hated to think of her father wandering the lands, untethered from life. She especially hated to consider that she might one day encounter the final remnants of who he'd been in battle at the Veils.

She shook her head to dislodge the image of her father. "Are you sure about that? The Fae are all about honor and it wouldn't be honorable to walk away from the Veils after having made the commitment."

"It also wouldn't be honorable to leave behind a mate who will either suicide or Fade."

"Basically, what you're saying is that a Guardian with a mate can have no honor, for they would lose it no matter which way they chose. That being the case, we should really go."

"That's not what I meant."

"But it's the truth. My mother lost her honor in doing the honorable thing and choosing to die upon the Veils. Yet if she'd chosen my father and me, she would have lost her honor anyway, for doing right by her mate and child."

"If you want to look at it that way. My point is you should find out. Take a chance, Kalina. What if he *is* your mate?"

An image of the man she would swear was now seated two tables away, and the child he'd held in his arms flashed through her head. She wasn't going through that. She wasn't going to risk it. Not for anything.

"Time to leave, Mitaru." She stood and rounded the table, heading for the door.

Perhaps it was fate that she had to pass by their table in order to reach the door. Perhaps it was simply bad luck.

She walked quickly and avoided looking at the table or the men seated there as she walked by.

It was because she wasn't watching, though, that she was taken off guard when a chair was shoved directly into her path, knocking her off course.

She stumbled into their table, directly across from the Fae she was desperate to avoid.

He looked up and there was a long, timeless moment of eternity, when she was lost in a sea of green.

"Kalina, you okay?" Mitaru grabbed her arm and pulled her back a step, breaking the spell and waking her to the disaster that her life had just become.

"Yes. I'm fine. I have to go." She broke free from Mitaru's hold and bolted for the door.

"nother round?" Tarek asked.

"Why not?" Nako exclaimed.

"I'm in," Thorne said.

"Great!" Tarek shoved back his chair and the next thing Thorne knew, a gorgeous Fae stumbled into their table right across from him.

She caught herself against the table's surface and looked up.

Thorne had a moment to register the sheer beauty of her eyes, their color somewhere between a bright pink and a soft purple, then there was nothing but the throb of his heartbeat and an endless moment during which he would swear he could hear her soul calling to his.

Someone said something and the spell was broken.

She jerked back, said something to the man beside her, then rushed away.

"Wait!" Thorne leapt to his feet and raced after her, ignoring the exclamations and questions at his back.

When he burst from the tavern, he found the woman and the male Fae she'd been with arguing.

"You can't just run away from this," the male Fae was saying.

"Watch me."

Thorne hurried forward. "Please. Don't run. Just talk to me. Who are you? What was that?"

The woman slowly turned to face him, a look of resignation and sorrow on her face.

The minute their eyes met, he felt that same sense of timelessness and of being pulled deeper into some destiny he'd known nothing about until moments before.

"Who are you?" he asked again.

She didn't answer.

"I'm Mitaru Verushi," the male Fae standing at her side said. "And this is Kalina Wyendeh."

"You're Guardians," Thorne said with some surprise as he finally registered the mark of a Guardian-born on Kalina's face.

"As are you."

Everything inside Thorne tightened and expanded all at once at the sound of her voice, one he would swear he'd heard before.

It felt as if his entire soul was leaning toward her, drinking her in. "Yes. My name is Thorne Evaria and I serve the Veils of the East."

"We serve those of the West," Mitaru said

This would explain how they'd never met until now.

"Why do I feel such a connection to you?" Thorne asked. "It can't be a matebond. We're Guardians. So, what is it?"

Mitaru let out a scoffing sound.

Kalina sent him a glare and Thorne read something in that glare he'd always believed impossible.

"What's going on, Thorne?" Tarek came up to stand on one side of him, Nako on the other.

Thorne didn't answer. He was too busy staring at Kalina as the world faded away. *Are we mates?* He focused and sent the message arrowing toward her in the only way he knew to see if they were truly mates or not.

If they were, a path would have opened between the two of them the moment they met.

Kalina jerked and her eyes flew to his.

By the fates, how had this happened?

They were Guardians, destined to step into eternity alone.

I can't, her voice whispered in his head. *I am sorry. This is not meant to be. We may be mates, but we are also Guardians. We must be true to the cause, to the Veils, to our destiny.*

She was right, but it hurt in ways he would never have imagined it could. He'd never wanted a mate, never expected one, yet now faced with her beauty and presence and the sound of her voice, the pain filled every pore of his being and left him hollowed out.

You're right, I know. But we can get to know each other, right? Spend time together while we're here? I assume you're in Eonara for the training. Give us the gift of these two days.

We'll be far from each other, serving the Veils once more, soon enough.

*K*alina knew it was a terrible idea. To even speak to him was to strengthen both the path and their bond and thus, was a terrible risk. To spend time with him was an even greater one. If their bond grew too strong, they might not have the strength of will to embrace their duty as Guardians of the Veil.

Yet, she could not find it in herself to deny him. To deny herself.

No touching. And no more talking this way. We speak out loud and we do everything we can to keep this bond weak.

Agreed, he answered. *Turning our backs on the bond, more even than sacrificing ourselves on the Veils, will be our true and final gift to Faerie.*

CHAPTER 10

By the next day, Thorne was already regretting their agreement.

Both Tarek and Nako thought he was making a mistake.

They had argued with him long into the night.

"Fight for your mate, Thorne," Tarek had exclaimed.

"He's right," Nako had said. "There is no greater gift for a Fae than to find his or her fated mate. You need to try to convince her. Just try."

Thorne had spent the night thinking of their arguments and what he could say to Kalina to convince her.

The problem was he wasn't even sure he wanted to.

His had spent his entire life expecting to become a Guardian, to serve the Veils of Faerie, and now that he knew he had a mate, he wasn't sure that dream needed to change.

After all, his mate was also a Guardian of the Veils. From what he could tell, they shared a sense of honor and duty which meant they were undoubtedly well-matched.

He fell asleep agonizing over the situation and woke restless and eager to spend the day with the mate that destiny would deny him.

They met outside the Inn of Osayede, where the Guardians of the West were staying.

Thorne half expected Mitaru to be with her, but Kalina waited alone. This was excellent news because it had taken all of Thorne's strength the night before to allow the two to leave the tavern together.

The feral part of his soul had roared for the blood of the Fae who dared accompany his mate, who dared brush against her, touch her arm in a friendly intimacy Thorne wanted for himself.

He wasn't sure he could have been civil this morning if the other Fae had shown up with her.

Thorne knew the second Kalina caught sight of him approaching. She straightened from where she'd been leaning against the rail at the front of the inn, and for a split second, the path connecting the two of them throbbed with an intensity of emotion before Kalina sealed it off at her end.

Thorne stopped in front of her and stared, drinking her in.

She was beautiful, of course. All the Fae were.

But this was more.

Her dark skin glowed with vitality and youth, though Thorne knew she had to be at least six hundred if she was in Tarek's generation of Guardians and would be over a thousand if she was in Thorne's.

Her eyes shone with a light only another Fae could see. A light that beckoned with thousands of secrets from an untarnished soul.

He wanted to reach out and touch her, take her hand, kiss her cheek, pull her into his arms, but he had agreed there would be no touching.

So he stayed his distance and murmured her name, the sound of it bringing peace to his soul. "Kalina."

She did not smile, simply said his name in return. "Thorne."

"Shall we walk?"

She inclined her head and joined him.

They walked side-by-side, instinctively leaving a space between them so there would be no accidental touches, and wandered without any destination in mind, content simply to be together.

They'd been walking for a while before Kalina finally spoke again. "Tell me about yourself."

So Thorne did.

He told her of his younger brother, Tarek, who had just joined him as a Guardian a hundred years before.

He spoke to her of his best friend, Nako, who had joined the Guardians with him, and would walk by his side into their destiny.

He shared amusing anecdotes of growing up with Nako and Tarek and coaxed Kalina into sharing about her life as well.

Her stories were all about her role as a Guardian, fighting the Sorenalaya and guarding the Veil. When pressed, she eventually shared stories of training with Mitaru and traveling with him and his sisters throughout Faerie and the mortal realms.

It wasn't until their second day together that they shared deeper secrets. Thorne spoke to her about his parents, who had been both proud and devastated to have two Guardian sons and who had succumbed to old age just sixteen years past.

He spoke of his conflicting emotions regarding their loss. Relief that they would not have to witness his passing, and terrible grief. Grief for himself, but more for Tarek, who would be alone once Thorne's tenure as a Guardian came to its inevitable end.

It was only after he had shared about his parents that Kalina finally shared the story of hers and their doomed romance.

It was in that moment that Thorne understood

there was nothing he could say that would convince her to give their mating a chance. She would never risk repeating her mother's mistakes.

So be it.

He had already resigned himself to the possibility that they might never bond in truth and that these two days might be their only days together. Hearing her speak of her mother's decisions and the lasting consequences of them, he said goodbye to any dreams he might have had otherwise.

He asked questions about Mitaru and was somewhat soothed to know from her response that she did not see the other Fae in any romantic light. He was her best friend and her companion and they had a bond, it was true, but it was not sexual in nature.

This soothed the feral Fae inside and Thorne thought perhaps he could live with their parting, knowing she did not leave him for another Fae, but for the good of all of Faerie.

It seemed to Kalina to be the vast hand of fate that she and Thorne were not just Guardians, but that they were both of the same generation, set to perish upon the Veils in four hundred years' time.

Neither would have to live in a world without the other and both could take comfort in knowing their souls might find one another when they passed from this life to the next.

Somehow, she was certain, their souls were now linked, even though they had not undergone any of the Fae rituals to tie them together.

"We will not be alone," Thorne murmured as he stared into her eyes the evening of their second day together.

They had spent the past two days wandering the city of Eonara, at times pausing to admire a piece of pottery or jewelry at an artisan stand or to eat a meal at a restaurant in the heart of the city.

"No," she said quietly. "No matter how far we travel from each other, we will always be together."

"Hold out your hand," he said.

She hesitated.

"I won't touch it. Just please hold it out."

She dragged in a breath for courage, then held out her right hand.

Without touching her wrist, he carefully attached something around it, then stepped back.

Kalina's eyes widened when she saw the bracelet lying there.

They had seen it at an artisan stand the day before. She had fallen in love with it, though she hadn't asked about it or lingered near it, for she'd been certain it would cost more than she was willing to pay.

It was an absolute work of art.

Silver discs with tiny threads of amber etched upon their surface were connected together by the finest links of silver.

The amber was woven into each disk in the pattern of one of the oldest of Fae languages.

She ran her thumb over the amber and it seemed to warm against her skin.

"The amber holds a tiny piece of our bond—your life force and mine mixed together," Thorne said. "It's just a small spell to help you remember that no matter how alone you feel, no matter how many years pass or how far apart we travel, you will always carry me with you. Even in four hundred years time, when we walk into eternity half a world apart, I will be there, walking at your side."

For Kalina, a Fae who had no use for romance, nor any need of it in her life, it was an extraordinary moment, deeply romantic and achingly pure.

She was stunned at the gesture and at the deep well of respect and love she saw shining from Thorne's eyes.

He would not try to convince her that they should turn their back on Faerie, but instead would be with her, however he could, and in so doing, they would in fact, be mated in every way but deed.

"Thorne," she whispered, overwhelmed at the beauty of the moment and swamped with love for this Fae she'd only met a couple days before, yet knew to the depths of his soul.

"I know, Kalina mine. We will meet again. If not in this lifetime, most definitely in the next." He gave her a deep bow of respect, then turned and walked away, leaving her at the center of the courtyard outside the Inn of Osayede, her heart on her wrist and her soul yearning for more.

And so, the centuries passed.

For Thorne, every leave-taking was as hard as the first, when he'd walked away with the sense of having lost the most important battle of his life, ash in his throat and on his tongue.

Four centuries too early, he'd thought. The taste of ash was not supposed to come until it was time to burn for Faerie.

Though Kalina and Thorne did their best to avoid meeting each other in the years that followed, it was a losing battle.

As mates, they were drawn to each other and over hundreds of years, built up memories they would take into eternity with gratitude and honor.

They stayed apart as long as they could, then when the yearning became too much, every ten or fifteen years, they would arrange to meet somewhere between the East and the West, middle ground from where they each served.

They were extremely careful, every time, never to touch.

Not even the brush of a single finger could be allowed, out of fear they might unleash the roar of their matebond.

Whenever they met, they walked apart as they had that first day together in Eonara. The space between them eventually evolved into space enough for two other Fae, for the closer they stood to each other, the greater the pull.

As time went on and that pull became an aching throb that was almost impossible to resist, Kalina began to bring Mitaru with her to their meetings, and Thorne, Tarek and Nako.

The three served as barriers—chaperones almost— and when the time inevitably came for them to part once more, they were instrumental in helping Kalina and Thorne maintain their sanity.

They became five comrades in arms, all five of them

mourning each time Kalina and Thorne had to walk away from each other.

It was over the course of these many centuries that Kalina began to feel closer to her long-lost parents again.

She began to understand the pull her mother would have felt and ultimately, the devastating choices she had faced. If Mitaru was right and her parents had been fated mates, Kalina could only feel a vast sense of pity and sorrow for their sake.

They had made choices different from the ones Kalina made, but she couldn't say anymore that those choices were any less valid than her own.

Her parents had undoubtedly done the best they could when the winds of fate had changed their lives forever.

And so the years passed, in joy and in sorrow, as Kalina and Thorne met and parted again and again.

Until finally the day came when Kalina stood inside the Guardian Compound of the Western Veils and felt the bond strengthen and throb with the nearness of her mate.

Though she could barely believe it, *he was coming to her.*

Everything after that came in flashes.

Running headlong toward her love.

Thorne swinging her around in his arms.

Touching her as he'd never done before.
Introducing him to her Commander.
Then to her fellow Guardians.
Then to those of her unit.
Taking him on a tour of the compound.
Leading him to the Falls of Dyagonin.
Spending yet one more glorious day together.
Until they were called to return.

CHAPTER 11

Kalina knew the news would not be good.

At best, they would be allowed to stay together, but forbidden to complete their mating.

At worst, Thorne would be sent back to the Western Veils and they would be faced with a choice: accept the destiny that had been written for them long ago and die half a world away from each other, or walk away, leaving the fate of the Fae in the balance.

They had spent four hundred years preparing to burn upon the Veils half a world away from each other. Yet now that they'd touched, now that Thorne was here in her compound, that choice was a bitter one.

Still, she knew, in her heart of hearts, no matter how

strong their love or their aversion to that first choice, neither of them could live with walking away.

When they reached the administrative building, instead of being directed to the Commander's office once more, they were led toward the back of the building where the Fae courts convened.

Kalina's heart pounded as she registered what that meant.

Not just the Commander then.

Today, they would face a Tribunal.

Thorne stiffened at her side. Though his tour had not included the administrative building, he clearly understood this wasn't good.

His hand tightened on hers and she knew he had to be raging at the perceived threat to his mate.

"Peace, Thorne," she whispered. "We go into whatever awaits us together."

His hand relaxed and he stroked his thumb across the palm of her hand, causing fire to spread outward from that simple connection.

She caught her breath and closed her eyes, allowing the fire to swamp through her system and then dissipate.

They arrived outside the doors of the Breaiga, the Fae Court of the Western Veil.

Nadim turned to look at Kalina.

She nodded and he gestured to the Guardians stationed on either side of the doors.

They flung them open and Kalina and Thorne strode down the center aisle toward where the Tribunal waited.

The Tribunal was typically made up of three Commanders and two Guardian representatives.

For High Crimes, a royal might sit upon the Tribunal.

A Fae could gauge how serious their crimes by the individuals chosen for their Tribunal. How high the Guardians ranked, how important the Commanders, how close to the Queen the royals were.

In all her years as a Guardian, though, Kalina had never heard of more than one royal sitting upon any Tribunal, which was why her steps faltered when she saw who was seated on the raised Tribunal dais.

At opposite ends, two Commanders sat. One was Commander Agarra, so she assumed the other commander was probably Thorne's.

This was not unusual. In fact, it was customary for the Commander of those on trial to serve on their Tribunal.

What wasn't customary was for the Queen herself to preside over the Tribunal or for her two daughters, Astra and Glory, to serve with her.

This wasn't good.

Kalina's hand tightened on Thorne's as her anxiety spiked.

Not one, not two, but *three* royals on their Tribunal and zero Guardians to speak on their behalf.

This was *not* good.

They must have all used Fae magic to arrive here so quickly, which was also not a good sign.

It spoke of urgency and of gravitas.

A quick glance into the upper balconies revealed they were packed with Guardians from the Western Veil.

That was also not good.

It showed her fellow Guardians believed she would need their support.

"Step forward, Guardians." Queen Naira, who was seated at the center of the Tribunal beckoned them closer.

Gathering her courage, Kalina walked with Thorne to the center of the courtroom and faced the Tribunal.

Silence fell and with it a stillness that settled like a weight upon them.

"I understand you two have known you were fated mates for four hundred years. Is that correct?" The queen asked.

"Yes, my queen," Kalina and Thorne said together.

"And why is it you have not requested to be released from your bonds as Guardians?"

"We do not wish to walk away from our duty," Kalina said.

"We both feel strongly this is our path, Queen Naira," Thorne said.

"So strongly you would deny the matebond, the greatest gift any Fae has ever known?"

"We do not deny the matebond," Kalina protested. "We acknowledge it exists without allowing it free reign. We made this choice long ago so as not to sever our prior bonds to the Veils of Faerie and to the Guardians with whom we serve."

"A choice you made four hundred years ago," the Queen repeated solemnly. "And is that still the choice you would make today, Guardian Evaria?"

The Fae Queen was as insightful as Thorne had always heard. She sensed his doubts, but perhaps not the full depth of his resolution.

Thorne searched for the right words to explain. "The truth is, Queen Naira, we made this choice four hundred years ago, yes, but we also made it six months ago and again four weeks ago. We even made it on the bridge six hours ago when I arrived here at the Western compound and yet again, not fifteen minutes ago when we were summoned here.

"Every time we have met over the past four hundred years, we have made that choice again, deliberately, not just for the good of Faerie, but for each other as well, for we are Guardian-born.

"We were made for this purpose, to serve the Veils of Faerie and that is both a sacrifice and an honor.

"These past four hundred years have been bitter-sweet. We have found each other and have gained both peace and sorrow in the finding." He stroked his thumb across Kalina's palm, then shook her hand a little, causing the bracelet he'd given her so many centuries before to slip down her wrist into the gap between their hands. He pressed their palms together, trapping the links of the bracelet between them, and felt the amber heat against their skin.

"So, to answer your question, Queen Naira, we have already made that choice a hundred times this day, over and over again throughout the long hours we spent together, waiting for your summons."

Silence fell once more as the Tribunal processed his words.

The Queen made a discreet motion to Princess Astra on her right.

"The Fae are indebted to all of our Guardian Forces," Princess Astra said. "It is expected that

Guardians will willingly sacrifice their lives for the good of Faerie and while we acknowledge the sacrifice, we do not perhaps appreciate it as much as we should, for it is not just your physical lives you offer in service to Faerie.

"All Guardians abandon the hope of finding their fated mates when they pledge themselves to the Veils. It is not something we speak of or even think about—what it means to deny the potential for a matebond. We assume those who are accepted as Guardians were meant to be alone, but now that truth has been laid bare. Perhaps instead it is simply that Guardians have not been allowed the freedom to search.

"And so, we Fae have not only denied generations of Guardians their lives, but we have also denied them the potential for love."

"That is not true," Kalina said, startling Thorne and the entirety of the Tribunal. "I apologize for interrupting, Princess Astra, but I have known love and I knew it long before I met Thorne. I have found a family among the Guardians and I have found a home. We may not be bonded to one another in matebonds, but we have bonds nonetheless and I would daresay not a single Guardian would claim any regret should you ask him or her."

The sound of drumming feet filled the court chambers and brought warmth to Thorne's heart. The

Guardians were showing without saying a word that they stood with Kalina and Thorne and that they agreed with her statement.

They had no regrets.

Astra inclined her head in acknowledgment and said, "I stand corrected, Guardian Wyendeh. I have no desire to undermine the incredible sacrifice that each Guardian offers the Fae. Still, it is one thing to enter as a Guardian and to know that you will never meet your fated mate as a result. It is something else entirely for that claim to be revealed a lie and for you to be forced to deny your matebond for hundreds of years in service to the Fae. That you have both chosen this path is a true testament to your honor and integrity."

She paused and glanced to her right, where Commander Agarra was seated.

Commander Agarra gave a short nod in agreement.

Princess Astra then leaned forward, looked to her left and received nods from Princess Glory and from Commander Helier.

She then settled back in her chair and waited.

Finally, Queen Naira gave the tiniest of nods, so minuscule if Thorne hadn't been looking for it, he would have missed it.

Princess Astra began to speak again.

"It appears fate itself has conspired to bring these events to pass. When we consider them together—

that the two of you met at all, that you were both strong enough to deny the matebond for hundreds of years, that the Seers insisted this is where Thorne Evaria had to be in the final days leading up to the Ceremony of the Veils—it becomes increasingly clear. We were all on this path, though we knew it not.

"More importantly, it is not the purview of the Fae to deny what Fate has decreed. For better or for worse, you two are destined mates.

"It is true that had we discovered this fact four hundred years ago or even a year ago, the decisions of this Tribunal would be different. Unfortunately, today is too late, when we have already had to call upon the Reserves, to make any other choice.

"Guardian Wyendeh and Guardian Evaria, we acknowledge your matebond, and we welcome you as the first of your kind, *mated* Guardians of the Veil."

Kalina's breath caught in her throat as the bond between her and Thorne came to life with throbbing force.

Gratitude and relief and a searing feeling of joy whipped through the bond, arching from Kalina to

Thorne and back to her, a wild emotional ride whose sheer magnitude nearly sent her to her knees.

Princess Astra began to speak again and Kalina's focus snapped back.

"We are here now," Princess Astra said, "—*all of us* are here now—" She raised her arms to indicate the Fae Guardians in the balconies above. "—to serve as witnesses to the matebond ceremony of two of our brightest stars. Guardians, make your vows please."

As Kalina faced Thorne, and gazed up into his brilliant, green eyes, she was amazed to realize she had no fears.

Somehow, in the four centuries of finding and yearning for her mate, they had all evaporated. She no longer feared what would happen if she bonded with a mate because she already had.

They may not have even touched before this morning and they may not yet have sealed their bond, but it was there, a brilliant, throbbing, constant companion of warmth and comfort and love.

"Kalina." Thorne cleared his throat. "I see eternity in your eyes and no matter the length of our days, I shall know peace so long as you are by my side. I offer you everything that I am, everything that I have been and everything I've yet to become, in this lifetime and in all the rest. With you, *for* you, I am my best self."

Kalina could barely see him through the tears in her

eyes. The words came from a deep well inside her she hadn't even known existed, from a hope she'd never dared to nurture or even acknowledge. "Thorne, my love, I see eternity in your eyes and no matter the length of our days, I shall know peace so long as you are by my side. I offer you everything that I am, everything that I have been and everything I've yet to become, in this lifetime and in all the rest. With you, *for* you, I am my best self."

Lost in Thorne's eyes, overwhelmed by the adoration and love traveling along their matebond, Kalina was only peripherally aware of Queen Naira standing, then slamming her hands together.

The chamber echoed with the sound of the queen's power as she swept one hand over the top of the other and flung her magic toward them.

It rained down upon them in tiny sparks of power, a royal blessing that made their skin sizzle with heat and their matebond throb in joy.

CHAPTER 12

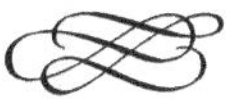

If she'd had ten thousand years to ponder the situation, Kalina would never have predicted the events that followed.

The queen had blessed their mating, then she and her daughters had left as quickly as they'd come, but not before granting Kalina and Thorne one final gift.

They were to be given twenty days and twenty nights to experience the full joy of their mating before they would be expected to present themselves for the Rituals of the Veils.

Twenty days and nights were a gift like none other for two Fae who had spent their lives expecting none.

Before they could be together though, they had to attend the celebration of their mating.

It lasted long into the night and as was tradition for

the Fae, Kalina and Thorne were kept apart for most of it.

Every once in a while, the Fae would conspire for the two to meet on the dance floor where they would exchange a heated embrace, only to have it ended by those same Fae, who would drag them apart and force them to opposite ends of the compound to continue celebrating.

Kalina and Thorne had touched each other for the very first time earlier that day, when he had caught her up in his arms and swung her around in pure joy, and all their touches since had been as innocent as the first.

Holding hands as they walked through the compound together.

Thorne helping her scramble up the boulder, then lifting her down again.

Kalina resting her head upon his shoulder, hugging him tight.

All those hours together and they had not kissed, not even once, perhaps out of fear that they'd unleash the true roar of their matebond.

This was how their very first kiss ended up happening in the middle of a Guardian compound, surrounded by their fellow Guardians and family.

To Thorne's surprise, Tarek had walked into the celebration about an hour after it began. He had swept them both into a bone-jarring hug, thrilled they were finally able to be together in truth.

When Thorne had demanded what he was doing there, Tarek had simply said, "Do you really think I would not request a transfer so that I could be there when my brother leaves this world? Technically, they haven't approved it yet, but I had leave coming to me and I wasn't above taking it. So I'm here and will be until the end."

Thorne had dragged Tarek back into his arms for another tight hug.

Grief had slid along the bond between Kalina and Thorne and her heart had broken for the brothers. However much grief Thorne felt in that moment, knowing he would be leaving Tarek behind, Kalina knew Tarek's grief had to be infinitely greater.

Then there was no more time for thinking because more Guardians descended upon them and dragged Thorne far from Kalina, which was when the celebration really took off.

The first time they were maneuvered onto the dance floor at the same time, Thorne didn't hesitate.

He swept Kalina into his arms and kissed her.

It was a kiss four hundred years in the making.

There was nothing slow or gentle about that first embrace.

Heat roared over them in a wave that rocked the

foundation of their world.

Kalina clutched Thorne's shoulders and tried desperately to get closer.

He wrapped one arm around her waist and the other around her shoulders, holding her still for his kiss.

The feel of his fingers gently stroking the nape of her neck sent heatwaves spiraling through her and she tried to climb him like a tree.

"All right, Kalina, that's enough of that." Mitaru's voice came to her as if from a fog, then an arm was around her waist and she was being dragged away.

The last she saw of Thorne was him struggling with his brother and a massive group of Guardians who were forcing him to back away from her.

And so it went.

She danced with practically every Guardian in attendance, male and female, but was only allowed fleeting touches with her mate.

And as the hours passed, the heat between them spiraled to massive heights until she could barely breathe for wanting him.

Finally, just as dawn was breaking through the horizon, her unit came for her and with Mitaru leading the way, took her outside the compound and into the woods where she rediscovered something she'd always known.

Her unit may not be hers by blood, but they were the best family a Fae could ever ask for.

Right alongside the bank of the River of Dyagonin, at the base of the pounding falls, they had used earth magic to create three walls and a canopy ceiling, all of it made from flowering vines.

Inside that beautiful green cave stood a mating bed for her and Thorne.

The four posts of the bed and its base were made of columns of vines and the mattress of leaves and flowers.

"Blessings upon your mating, Kalina," Mitaru said softly. "We wish you all the happiness in the realms."

"Blessings," the other Guardians murmured and then they were gone, leaving Kalina alone in her favorite place in all of Faerie.

Then, in a small pop of air magic, Thorne appeared at her side.

Kalina raised an eyebrow at him.

He shrugged. "Tarek's apparently been practicing."

Those were the last words they spoke for quite some time.

A bed of leaves and flowers might work for some couples, but for two Guardians who had waited four hundred years for this moment, believing it would never happen, the bed didn't stand a chance.

It collapsed beneath them almost immediately as

they rolled across its surface, kissing and struggling to remove each other's clothes.

They didn't even pause when it happened, just continued to wrestle with their clothes and kiss every bared part of the other they could reach.

Finally, after long moments of frustration interrupted by heated embraces and endless kisses, they were naked.

Thorne leapt for Kalina and took her down onto their collapsed bed of leaves and flowers, settling over her so that they were skin-to-skin everywhere.

She arched her back at the feel of all of him against all of her for the first time. Their skin heated where it touched and she relished the sensation.

The heat spiraled until she felt as if they were already burning upon the veils.

"Thorne," she whispered, bucking forcefully. "Please."

He caught her hands in his, pinning them to the ground on either side of her head, and laced his fingers with hers, trapping her bracelet between their wrists so that the amber came to vivid, heated life.

He settled his forehead against hers and staring into her eyes, slowly sank deep.

For one long, breathless moment, they hung there on a precipice, drowning in each other's eyes and the exquisite bliss of being together for the first time.

Then they began to move together in a rhythm as old as time.

Kalina had heard lovemaking between mates referred to as many things over the years: a dance, a merging, a fall, a journey, an evolution.

It turned out it was all of these and more.

It was an epic journey, an endless fall, a merging of souls, a dance between mates, an evolution into something greater together than what they'd been apart, and ultimately, a conflagration that consumed two souls and rebirthed them as one.

* * *

From the moment Thorne had seen Kalina and understood what she was to him, no other Fae could hold his interest.

Four hundred years of celibacy ended in a blaze so powerful, he wouldn't have been surprised if he'd burned to ash from the heat.

Had he known how intense and extraordinary a mating could be, he would never have survived four centuries of denying their bond.

A thousand years, *ten* thousand years, would not be

enough time to slake his burning need for his mate nor his desire to possess her in every way possible.

Yet, they only had twenty days and twenty nights to build a lifetime of memories.

He would have to make one day feel like ten thousand.

There, at the base of the pounding Falls of Dyagonin, four centuries from their first sighting of each other, with the roar of the water and their shared heartbeat in their ears and the sizzle of droplets from the falls landing on their heated skin, Kalina and Thorne finally sealed their matebond.

The days and nights that followed were filled with a joy Kalina had never known.

A bit of air magic delivered food to the river bank each day, something that made Thorne grin and shake his head. "Tarek must be teaching your unit all his tricks."

"You don't think Tarek's doing this himself?"

"He practically wiped himself out delivering me here. I doubt he's got the energy for daily food drops."

However it was happening, Kalina was grateful. It meant they didn't have to forage for food and could simply enjoy their time together.

And so their twenty days whittled down, just as their four hundred years had whittled down, bringing them ever closer to their destiny.

"I'll never regret becoming a Guardian," Kalina said, "not when it means having you at my side as we enter our final days."

Thorne kissed her thoroughly, which led to other things, much to Kalina's delight.

They didn't get back to that conversation until their final night together when Thorne said, "I will always be grateful that we met, that we had four hundred years to get to know one another, to really fall deeply in love with one another, and now, to be Guardian-mates at the end, together."

They spent their last night together making love, the passion they shared infinitely tender and sweet as their time together came to its inevitable end.

The next morning, they sat upon the boulder Kalina now considered theirs, wrapped in each other's arms, and watched as the rising sun set the waters of Dyag-onin afire.

CHAPTER 13

The Fae had a full ten-day set of rituals that led up to the Ceremony of the Veils. In the past, when Kalina had read about the rituals, they had seemed the perfect send-off for Guardians.

Then when she had participated in them five hundred years before, helping the older Guardians prepare for their final journey, she had believed that even more.

Now, though, when those ten days meant time away from Thorne, she wasn't so sure.

Until they reported for the first day and she discovered Shaliah had volunteered to take Norrick's place in his unit so that Thorne, who had been sent as Norrick's replacement, could join Kalina's.

This was a true blessing, for Kalina, Thorne and Mitaru already shared unshakable bonds, which allowed Thorne to slide seamlessly into her unit, almost as if he'd always served there.

And so, with Thorne and Mitaru and the rest of her unit at her side, Kalina participated in rituals that deepened the bonds they already shared.

Meditations in the woods.

Purifications beneath the Falls of Dyagonin.

Spirit walks.

Bathing rituals.

Anointing ceremonies.

And finally, the painting of the physical form with Fae symbols of power.

It was on the eleventh day that the Ceremony of the Veils took place.

As tradition dictated, the Ceremony began in Galandria, the closest village to the Western compound.

The Guardians of the Western Veil marched from the center of the village through the streets in formation. Each group of twenty-five represented a single unit and marched in columns of five by five.

Kalina's unit led the procession with the other four

units of their generation following. As the leader of her unit, Kalina marched at the center of the first row with Mitaru on her left and Thorne on her right.

As they walked through the streets of Galandria, Fae citizens stood on sidewalks and balconies, whispered prayers of thanksgiving and blessings and tossed flowers in their wake.

It was a three-hour walk from Galandria to the edge of the Western Compound and there were Fae lining the roads the entire way there.

As Kalina marched, she took comfort in the presence of her best friend and her mate and marveled at the beautiful turn her life had taken at the very last possible moment.

As they got closer to the Compound, the crowds grew. Family members and friends of her unit came into sight.

They wouldn't be allowed into the compound—only Guardians and Royals had those rights—but they were allowed to stand as witness outside it.

Kalina didn't search for her aunt or for anyone from her village for she knew none would be there. Instead, she searched for Luna and Zara and found them close to the gates to the Compound.

The two stood hand-in-hand, tears streaming down their faces.

They must have been standing there all night, to get

so close to where the Royal blessing would happen.

She heard a soft sound from Mitaru and knew he'd seen his sisters.

Then they were at the gate and Luna and Zara were no longer in her direct line of sight.

Instead, Kalina's attention was captured by Princess Astra, who stood on the rampart above the gate, waiting for their arrival.

Princess Astra, whom she and Mitaru had "rescued" at their Trials a thousand years before and who had most recently recognized Kalina's mating with Thorne.

From Trials to Tribunal to Sacrifice.

It seemed beautifully symbolic of Kalina and Thorne's journey, both apart and together.

"Welcome home, Guardians." Air magic lifted Princess Astra's voice and carried it on the wind so that it not only reached all the Guardians and witnesses standing at the gates, but traveled all the way to Galandria so witnesses there could hear it too.

"You have gifted the Fae with a thousand years of service and we are grateful. Today, we are here to honor your sacrifice and to bear witness as you step into eternity. Your journey does not end here, Guardians of the Veil, for you shall live in the hearts of the Fae forever."

As she spoke the ritual words, the tether that linked Kalina to each of the Guardians in her unit and beyond throbbed in recognition of their shared duty and honor.

"A thousand blessings be upon you." Princess Astra turned and walked down the stones stairs that led from the rampart to the ground below.

The gates opened to reveal two lines of Guardians, the next generation, standing facing each other, forming an Honor Guard, stretching as far as the eye could see, leading from one side of the Compound to the other.

Princess Astra walked to the front of the Honor Guard, Kahji at her side and the rest of the Royal Guard at her back. "To the Veil, Guardians."

She turned and led them through the Honor Guard.

It was a solemn procession as one hundred and twenty-five Guardians walked through the Honor Guard toward the gates on the opposite side of the Compound.

As they neared their destination, Thorne finally saw his brother.

Tarek stood at the end of the Honor Guard, waiting, eyes bright with grief and love.

Thorne's knees threatened to buckle at the sight, but he held strong and tried to convey with a simple look how grateful he was for Tarek's presence that day, how honored he felt to be his brother and how intensely proud he was of the honorable Fae Tarek had become.

For one long moment, it was as if time stood still.

Then he had passed where his brother stood and they were walking through the Northern gates and across the bridge Thorne had raced across a mere thirty-one days before.

They reached the other side of the gates and stopped. The lines of Guardians behind them slowly fanned out, so that Kalina stood front and center, Mitaru and Thorne on either side of her, then stretching slightly back and to either side, Guardians as far as the eyes could see.

Princess Astra waited until their formation was complete and the Guardians stood in stillness once more.

She placed her right hand over her heart and repeated her blessing. "Guardians of the Veil, from this day forward, you shall live in the hearts of the Fae forever."

She turned and walked toward the Veil. Her Guard

surrounded her and from one moment to the next, they went hazy then disappeared through the Veil.

They would be on the other side now, standing on mortal ground, projecting a glamour to shield Faerie and waiting to bear witness to the strengthening of the Western Veil.

As the Veil shimmered before them, Kalina could pick out tiny fractures in its surface.

It wouldn't be long now.

The Veil shuddered and rippled, flashing a glimpse of the mortal world and Princess Astra with her Guard on the other side.

The wail of Fae flutists filled the air and a soft buzz raised the hair at the nape of Kalina's neck.

Mitaru stood to her left and Thorne to her right.

Though grief hovered, Kalina held tight to her control.

The horns of Galadriel joined the flutes and the Guardians responded by clasping hands. When the flutes and horns reached a crescendo, there were no doubts, no questions, no hesitation.

It was simply a movement forward, not physically, but spiritually. Reaching out to the Veil, feeling the ripple of its power and potential, Kalina poured the entirety of her life force upon it.

Holding hands with her best friend on one side and her beloved on the other, Kalina leapt into eternity, dragging the rest of the Guardians with her.

CHAPTER 14

Fire.

That was all she knew.

An endless, burning, raging fire that swept through every pore and poured out into eternity.

To her left, Mitaru burned.

To her right, Thorne burned.

The grief that roared to life burned to ash, then raged forth again, only to burn once more.

And into the raging fire of destiny and hope and grief, there came a voice. "This is not the end. Not for the Fae. Not for the Guardians. And not for the Veils. It is a beginning."

The fire burned away in a flash of white light. So bright, it blinded and seared through bone. A different type of fire, but still they burned.

For a moment.

For eternity.

Then everything went dark.

The first sensation that returned to Kalina was the throb of the matebond, strong and comforting.

Next came the awareness of the hands holding her tight, the feel of Thorne's skin against her right hand and the feel of Mitaru's in her left.

Neither Fae had let go as the fire raged through them all.

Her sense of hearing returned with the sound of Thorne's voice. "Kalina."

She opened her eyes to see him leaning over her, eyes filled with concern. "Thorne?" A quick glance to her left showed Guardians as far as the eye could see, all down in a line. A glance to her right showed the same thing.

She turned her hand in Mitaru's and took comfort from the steady beat of his pulse, then slowly pulled her hand from his and struggled to a sitting position.

Thorne stood, then reached down and helped her up as well. He settled an arm around her waist and pulled her close so that her back rested against his chest as they stared at the Veil.

Or at the space where the Western Veil *should* be.

The Veils protected Faerie from the mortal world, shrouding pockets in space that would otherwise provide windows and doorways into the lands of Faerie.

Today, though, the Western Veil was down, revealing the incredibly large doorway that led to a college campus in a place called Lawrence, Kansas.

The other Guardians were beginning to stir, which was a good thing because Astra and Kahji and her entire Guardian force were on the mortal side of where the Veil had once stood and even Kalina could see their glamour had failed them.

Though Fae magic was much less predictable in the mortal worlds, the Fae had never had difficulty maintaining their glamour to hide their true selves.

With the Western Veil down, though, and the entirety of an unveiled Faerie at her back, Princess Astra fairly glowed with magic as she stood facing a crowd of humans who gawked and stared.

Something that had seemed a complete impossibility not five minutes before was now a terrible reality they had to face.

They'd been unveiled.

Faerie.

The Fae.

Princess Astra.

"This isn't good," Kalina said.

"We should join them," Thorne said. "They're terribly outnumbered."

Kalina took his hand in hers and together they passed through the doorway and entered the mortal realm.

Mitaru and the rest of Kalina's unit followed.

She imagined the rest of the Guardians would have joined them too if not for the shouted warnings.

"Sorenalaya! Sorenalaya!"

Kalina glanced back and saw Guardians forming a barrier on the Faerie side, facing off against the Sorenalaya.

She hesitated, torn between two loyalties, wishing to somehow be in both places so that she could protect the mortal world from the Sorenalaya *and* protect the Fae Princess from the mortals.

She stiffened her spine—surely the hundred Guardians on the Faerie side and the two hundred fifty of the next generations could hold back the tide—and turned her back on Faerie to face the mortal world and the consequences of their failure.

Within moments, it was obvious there would be no turning back the tide on this revelation for there was a sea of phones aimed their way, recording this disaster.

The hair lifted on the nape of her neck and something wrenched hard deep in her chest. She whirled to face Faerie once more, Thorne turning with her, and stared in horror.

The doorway to Faerie was still there, visible from this side, but a transparent shield had come down over it. That wrenching in her chest had been the Veils reconstructing into a barrier that felt so incredibly solid she wasn't sure they would be able to cross home again.

"Thorne," she whispered.

"Looks like we might be staying a while."

She leaned into his side, wondering if it was wrong to feel so grateful to have more time with her mate, especially given their current situation—trapped in a potentially hostile world full of mortals, where she and her fellow Guardians and the Royal Princess they had to protect had just been revealed as Fae. "At least we'll be together."

Thorne tightened his arm around her shoulders and dropped a kiss on her temple. "Forever, my love."

Together, they turned back to face the mortal world, ready to embrace whatever new destiny fate had in store for them.

Kalina, Thorne, the Fae princesses and countless other Fae are now trapped on the mortal side of the Veil. Read on for an excerpt from ASTRA, Book 1 of THE UNVEILED.

Mitaru's sisters, LUNA and ZARA, have been left behind in Faerie. Discover their stories in THE VEILED.

Kahji Nenzele kept his back to the Veil and his eyes on the chaos of the battle around them.

The Veil hid Faerie from mortal eyes, but it was the shield Princess Astra had constructed around the Fae that concealed them.

Despite the shield, as Captain of the Royal Guard, Kahji didn't trust that things wouldn't go wrong in a heartbeat, especially when the college campus he'd expected was instead a battlefield overrun by mortals attacking one another.

The only good news was that none of the mortals appeared to be carrying swords.

Instead, they used their bodies as weapons, hurtling

themselves at each other, hitting the ground and piling on top of one another before standing and beginning the process again.

It was the weirdest battle Kahji had ever seen. It seemed to move back and forth across the field in some strange pattern he couldn't quite discern.

In addition to the warriors on the field, Kahji also had to worry about the thousands of shouting mortals seated in tall structures on all four sides of them.

Kahji had a flash of memory from the far distant past: mortal gladiators, a giant colosseum, screaming spectators. It seemed the mortals had not changed much since the last time he had visited their realm.

At that moment, the mortal warriors all turned and barreled down the field toward them.

Kahji settled his hand on the hilt of his sword, ready to draw it should any of them manage to breach the shield Astra had constructed.

When they reached it, though, the runners blipped from one side to the other and continued running, seemingly unaware they had skipped an entire section of the field.

"Something's wrong," Astra exclaimed. "It's not working."

"What's not working?" Kahji winced as multiple warriors launched their bodies at another and they all went down in a pile of limbs.

"The Veil. It should have strengthened by now. It's getting worse."

Kahji's attention snapped back to the Veil.

She was right.

The fractures in the Veil were spreading, rather than closing as usual. "Perhaps the Guardians haven't sealed themselves to it yet."

"No. They *have*. Something's wrong."

As if in response to her statement, the ground trembled beneath them and a white light exploded from the Veil, lighting up the field and sending all the warriors there, both Fae and mortal, to the ground.

Kahji woke to a silence that blanketed the world.

He struggled to his knees and crawled to Princess Astra's side.

Her eyes snapped open. "It's down," she whispered.

"What is?"

"The Veil."

For the second time that day, Kahji's attention snapped to the Veil, or at least to where it should have been.

The doorway to Faerie was still there, but this time, there was no Veil shielding Faerie from mortal eyes.

Kahji leapt to his feet, then reached down and pulled Astra to hers.

A quick glance around them revealed that Astra's shield was down as well.

This was not good.

The doorway to Faerie was clearly exposed, providing *thousands* of mortals, both warriors on the field and spectators in the seats above, a view of Faerie few of their kind had ever seen.

Worse yet, the Fae's glamour had fallen, unveiling their true forms to the mortals.

Astra fairly glowed with the magic of Faerie, causing the mortals to fall silent at the sight of her.

"I can't access my magic, Kahji," Astra muttered.

"I know. I can't either."

"Without our glamour, we're completely exposed out here."

A man dressed in a black and white shirt, shoved to the front of the mortal warriors and stormed toward Kahji and Astra, shouting, "What do you think you're doing, interrupting the game like that? Get off the field!"

"We can't do that, Kahji, not with Faerie exposed like this."

"Guardians!" Kahji shouted. "Defend the Princess and guard the entrance to Faerie!"

The Royal Guard scrambled into position. Four Guardians surrounded the doorway to Faerie while Dyranel and Zanzor joined Kahji at Astra's side.

All seven of the Royal Guard drew their swords and pointed them at the mortals.

Kahji nudged the princess backward toward the Veil and snapped at the mortals advancing on them, "Stand back."

Find out what happens next in ASTRA.

THE SHENANIGANS SERIES

Shifter Shenanigans

Witchy Shenanigans

Full Moon Shenanigans

Hotel Shenanigans

Dragon Shenanigans

Undercover Shenanigans

Spooky Shenanigans

Holiday Shenanigans

Valentine Shenanigans

Lucky Shenanigans

STORIES OF THE VEIL

Guardians of the Veil

Astra

Glory

Luna

Zara

WICKED

No Rest for the Wicked

Wicked Is As Wicked Does

STORIES OF THE VEIL

THE UNVEILED

Astra | Glory

THE VEILED

Luna | Zara

WICKED DUET

WICKED

No Rest for the Wicked | Wicked Is As Wicked Does

ABOUT THE AUTHOR

WWW.PEPPERMCGRAW.COM

PEPPER MCGRAW is a *USA Today* Bestselling Author of paranormal romance. She hasn't met any paranormals to date, but she's sure that moment is just around the corner!

Pepper loves animals, especially cats, and spends her free time volunteering at local shelters and for Trap-Neuter-Release programs.

She's had the supreme honor of winning occasional head butts and meows from the local ferals in her neighborhood and has even convinced a few to come inside and adopt her as their own.

BB bookbub.com/authors/pepper-mcgraw
f facebook.com/ShenanigansSeries
g goodreads.com/peppermcgraw
instagram.com/peppermcgraw_author
tiktok.com/@peppermcgraw
twitter.com/peppermcgraw

www.ingramcontent.com/pod-product-compliance
Lightning Source LLC
Chambersburg PA
CBHW040226170726
48295CB00014B/820